Dear parents, caregivers, and educators:

If you want to get your child excited about reading, you've come to the right place! Ready-to-Read *GRAPHICS* is the perfect launchpad for emerging graphic novel readers.

All Ready-to-Read *GRAPHICS* books include the following:

★ **A how-to guide to reading graphic novels for first-time readers**

★ **Easy-to-follow panels to support reading comprehension**

★ **Accessible vocabulary to build your child's reading confidence**

★ **Compelling stories that star your child's favorite characters**

★ **Fresh, engaging illustrations that provide context and promote visual literacy**

Wherever your child may be on their reading journey, Ready-to-Read *GRAPHICS* will make them giggle, gasp, and want to keep reading more.

Blast off on this starry adventure . . . a universe of graphic novel reading awaits!

SPRINKLES AND SWIRLS

A Cool Day at the Pool

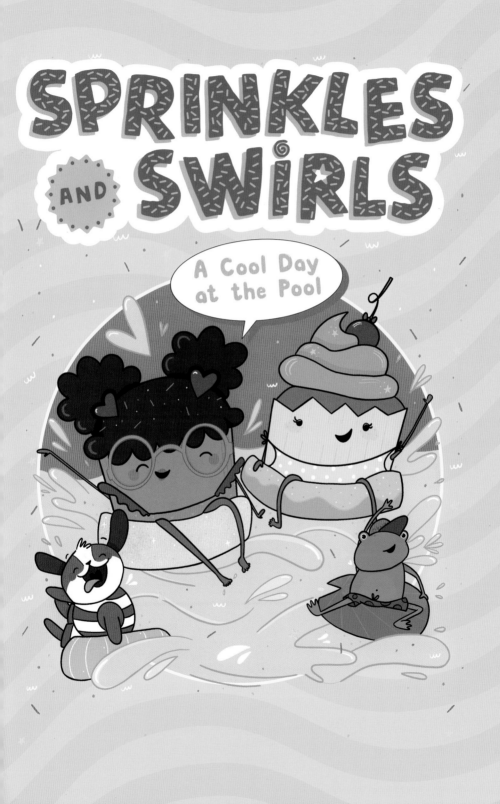

For Kathy, whose pool is always cool —L. S.

To Megan—you're the Sprinkles to my Swirls! —S. A.

SIMON SPOTLIGHT
An imprint of Simon & Schuster Children's Publishing Division
1230 Avenue of the Americas, New York, New York 10020
This Simon Spotlight edition May 2022
Text copyright © 2022 by Lola M. Schaefer
Illustrations copyright © 2022 by Savannah Allen
All rights reserved, including the right of reproduction in whole or in part in any form.
SIMON SPOTLIGHT, READY-TO-READ, and colophon are registered trademarks of
Simon & Schuster, Inc.
For information about special discounts for bulk purchases, please contact Simon & Schuster Special
Sales at 1-866-506-1949 or business@simonandschuster.com.
Manufactured in China 0222 SCP
2 4 6 8 10 9 7 5 3 1
Cataloging-in-Publication Data for this title is available from the Library of Congress.
ISBN 978-1-6659-0332-5 (hc)
ISBN 978-1-6659-0331-8 (pbk)
ISBN 978-1-6659-0333-2 (ebook)

SPRINKLES AND SWIRLS

A Cool Day at the Pool

Written by **LOLA M. SCHAEFER** ★ Illustrated by **SAVANNAH ALLEN**

Ready-to-Read *GRAPHICS*

Simon Spotlight
New York   London   Toronto   Sydney   New Delhi

HOW TO READ THIS BOOK

Sprinkles and Swirls are here to give you some tips on reading this book.

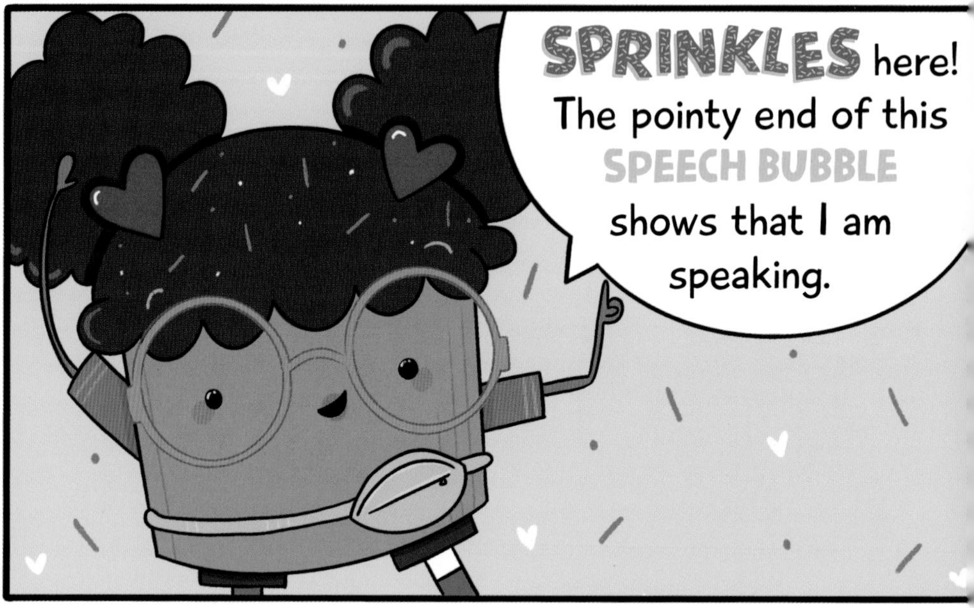
SPRINKLES here! The pointy end of this SPEECH BUBBLE shows that I am speaking.

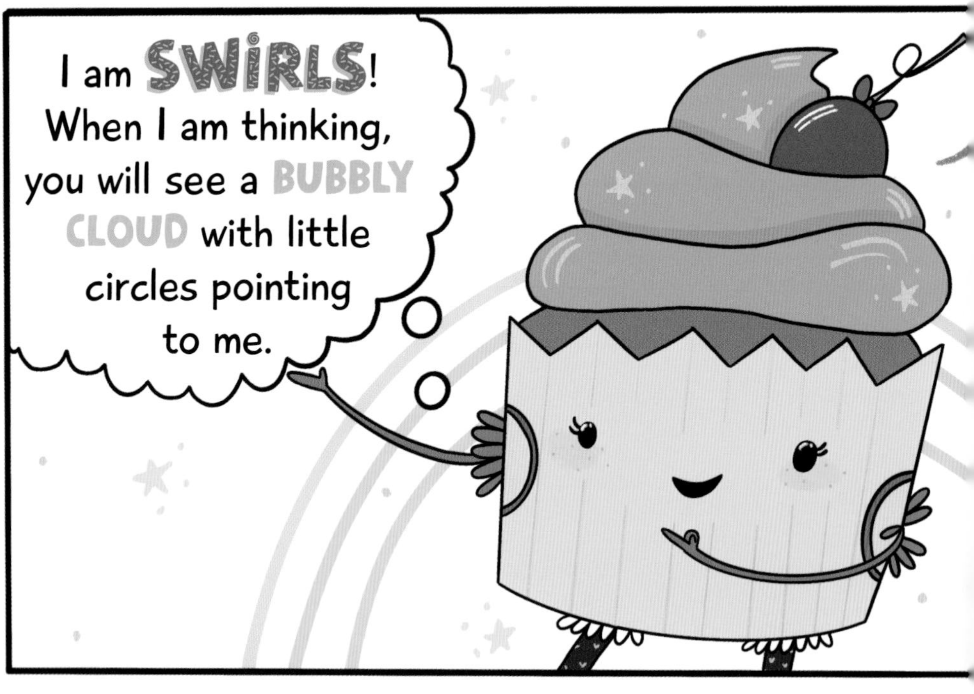
I am SWIRLS! When I am thinking, you will see a BUBBLY CLOUD with little circles pointing to me.

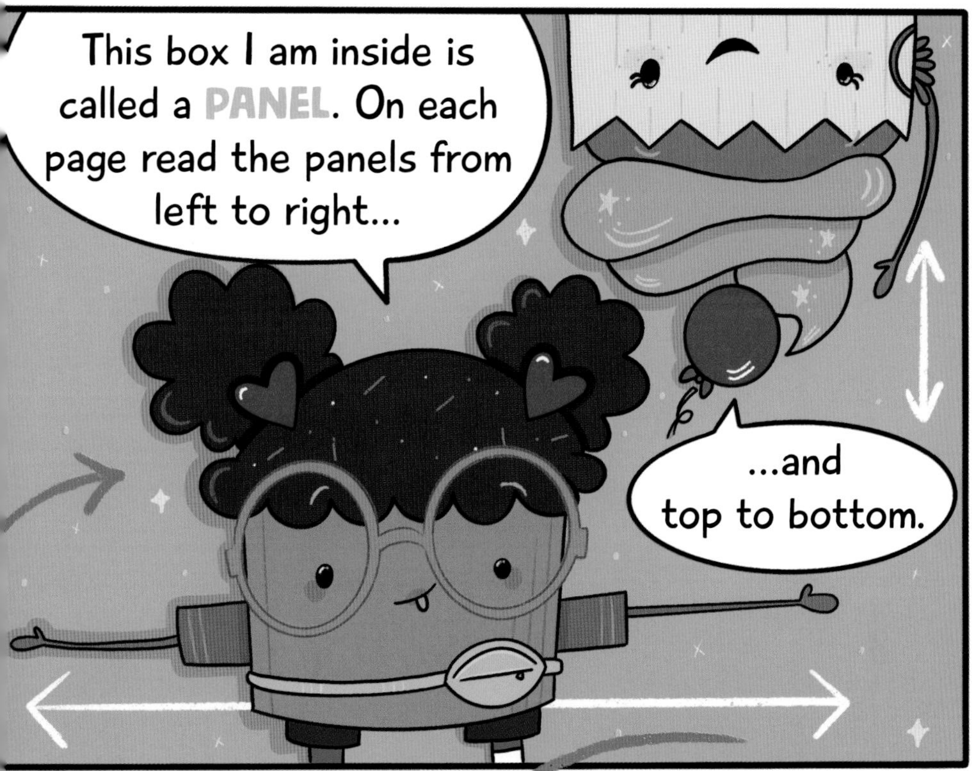
This box I am inside is called a PANEL. On each page read the panels from left to right...
...and top to bottom.

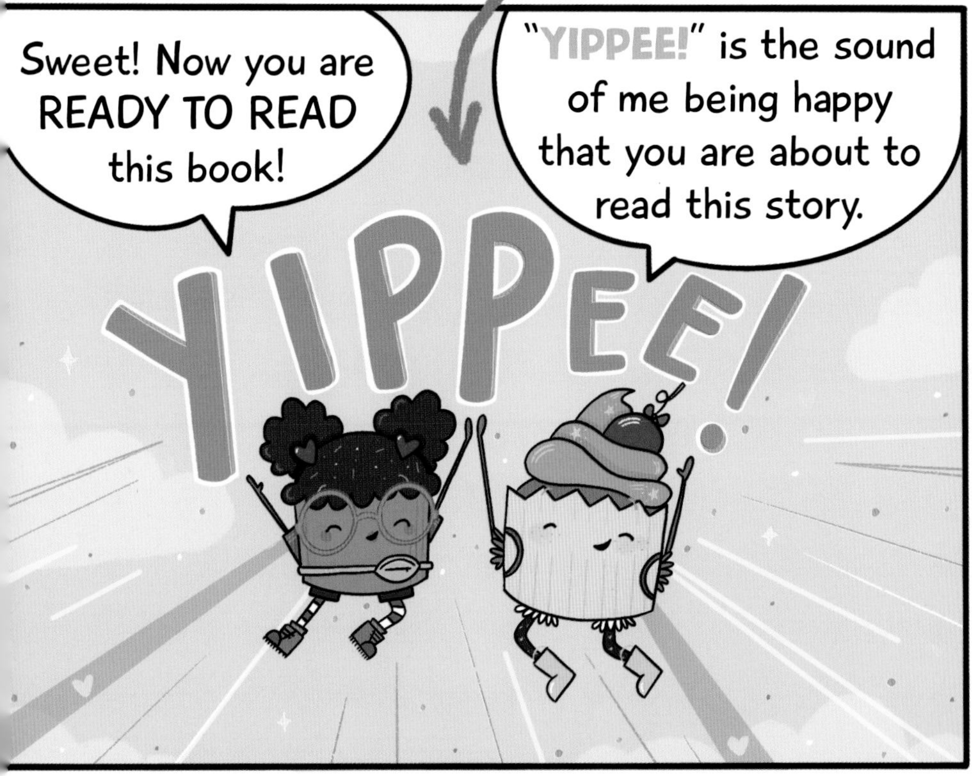
Sweet! Now you are READY TO READ this book!
"YIPPEE!" is the sound of me being happy that you are about to read this story.
YIPPEE!

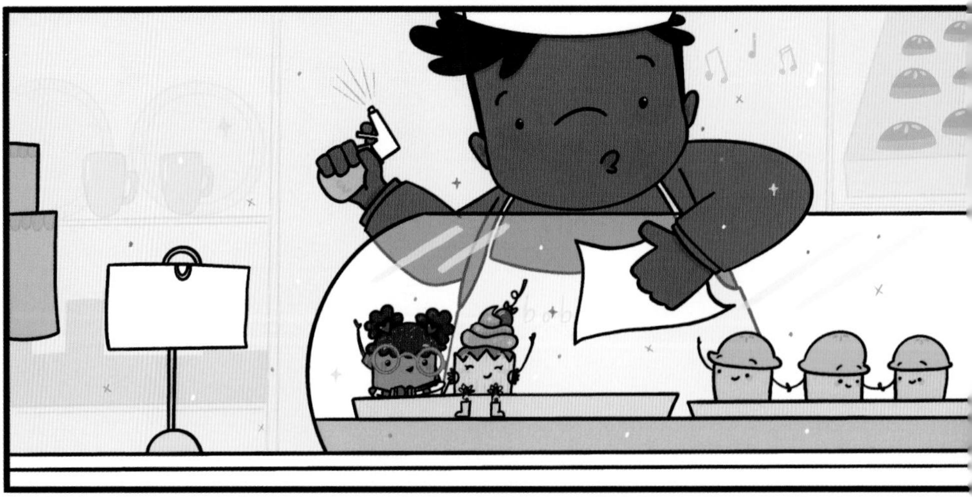

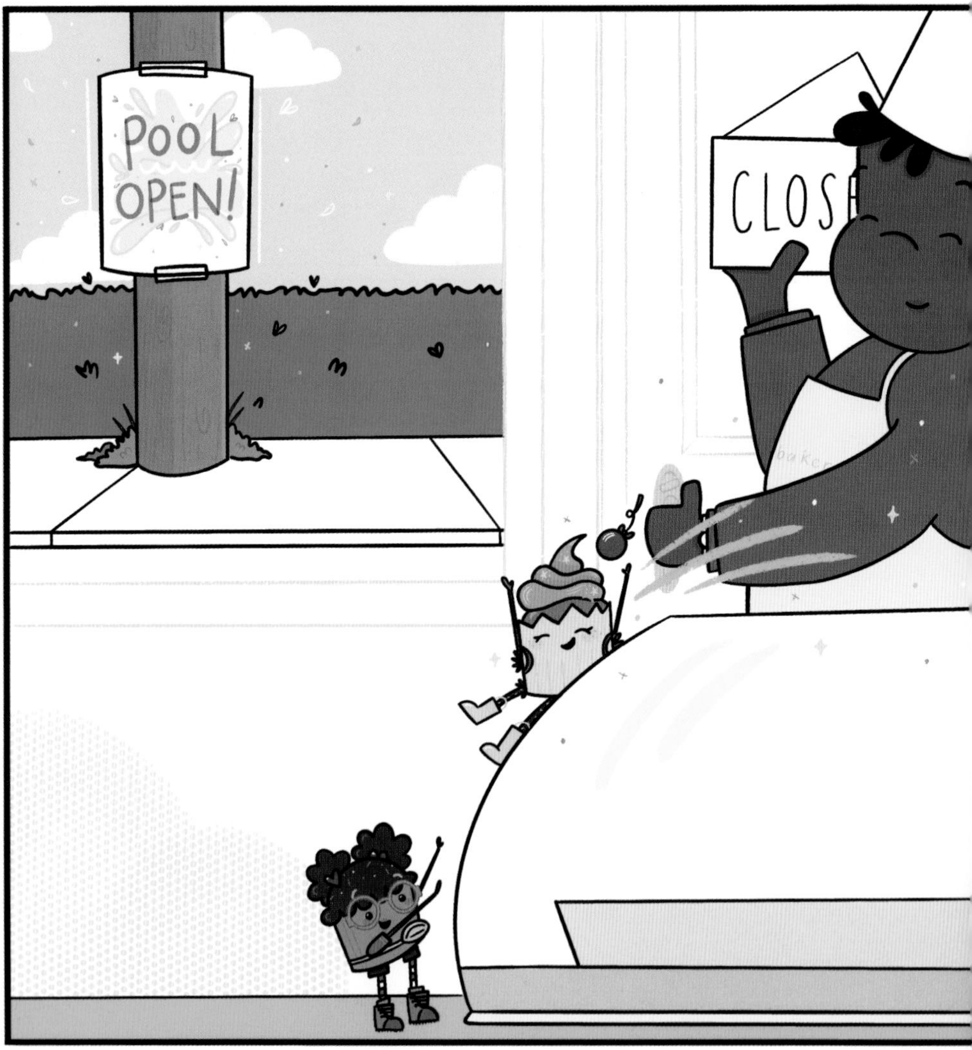
POOL
OPEN!
CLOS

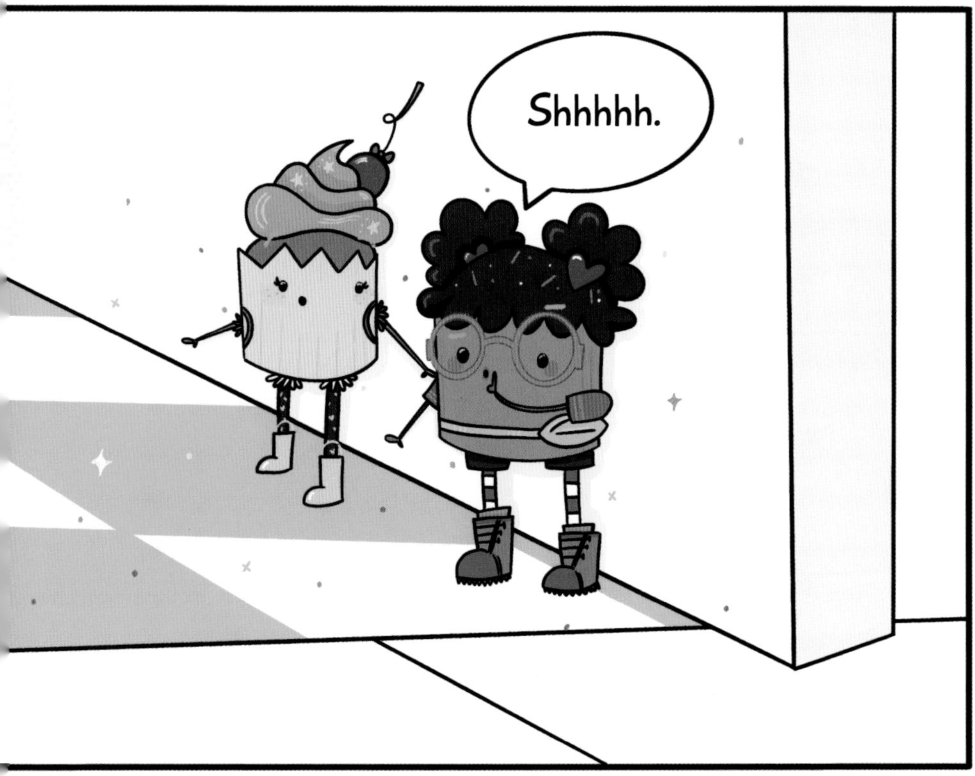
Shhhhh.

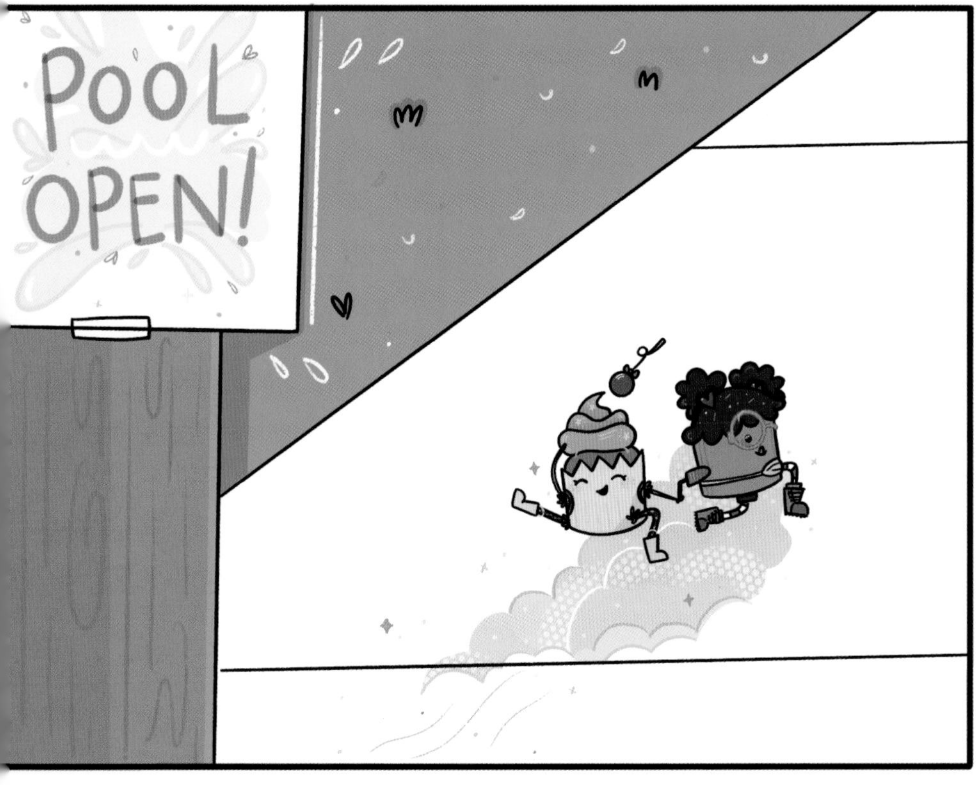
POOL OPEN!

Run, Swirls!

BUS STOP
Where are we going, Sprinkles?
Oh, you will love it!

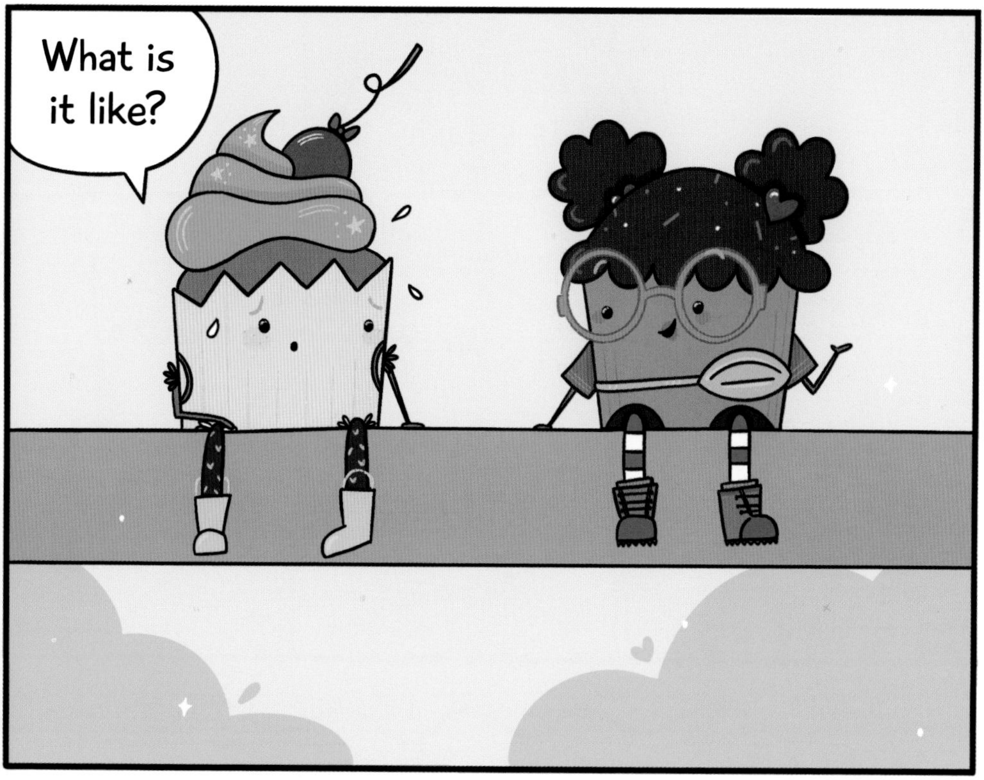
What is
it like?

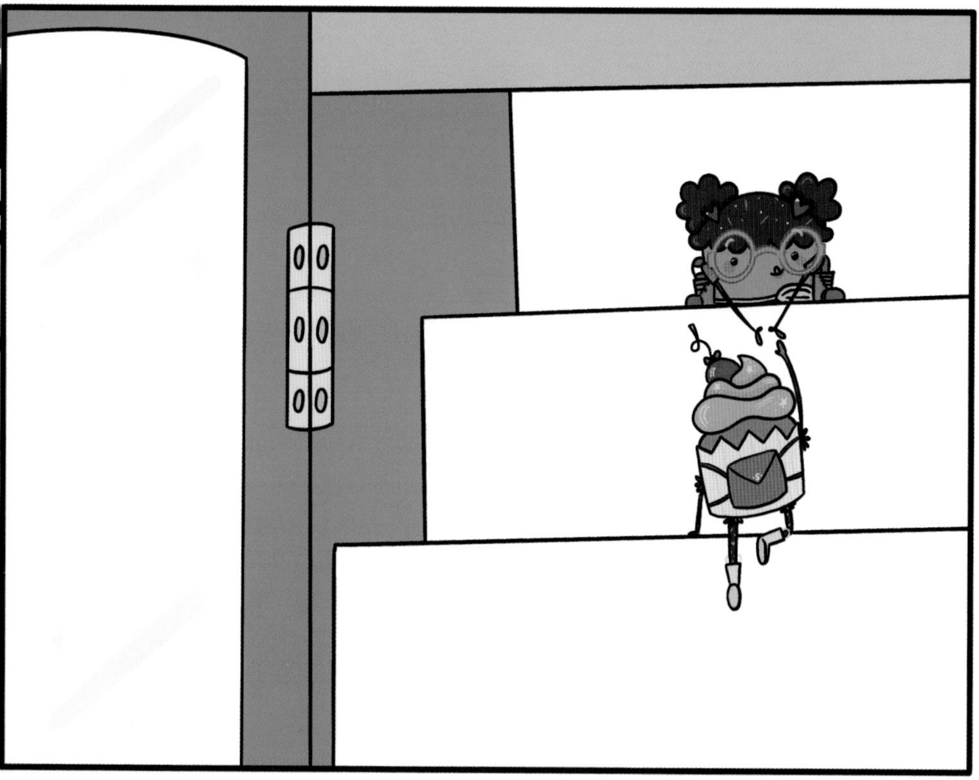

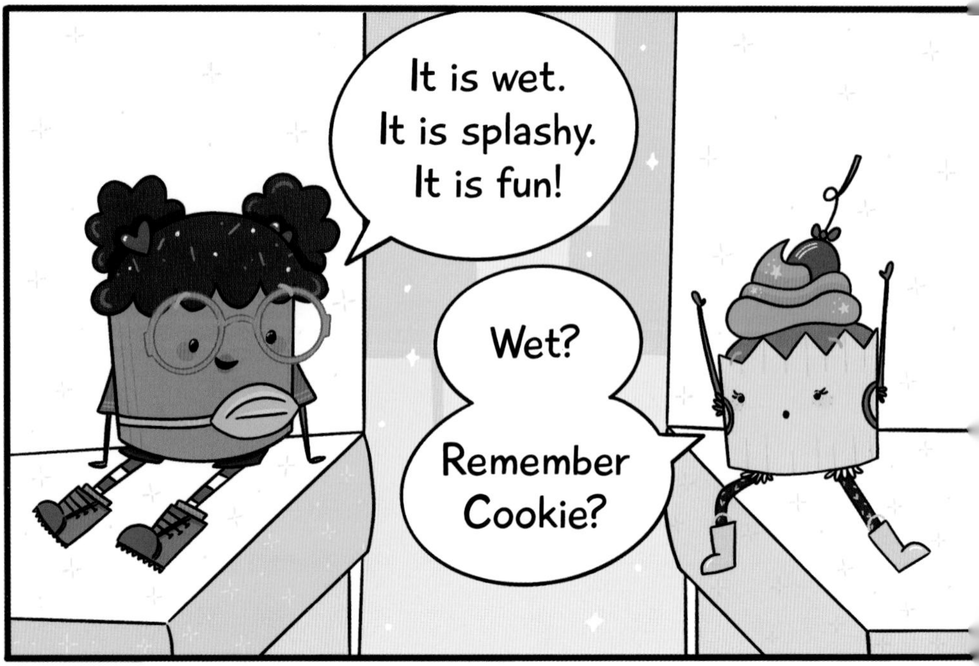
It is wet.
It is splashy.
It is fun!
Wet?
Remember
Cookie?

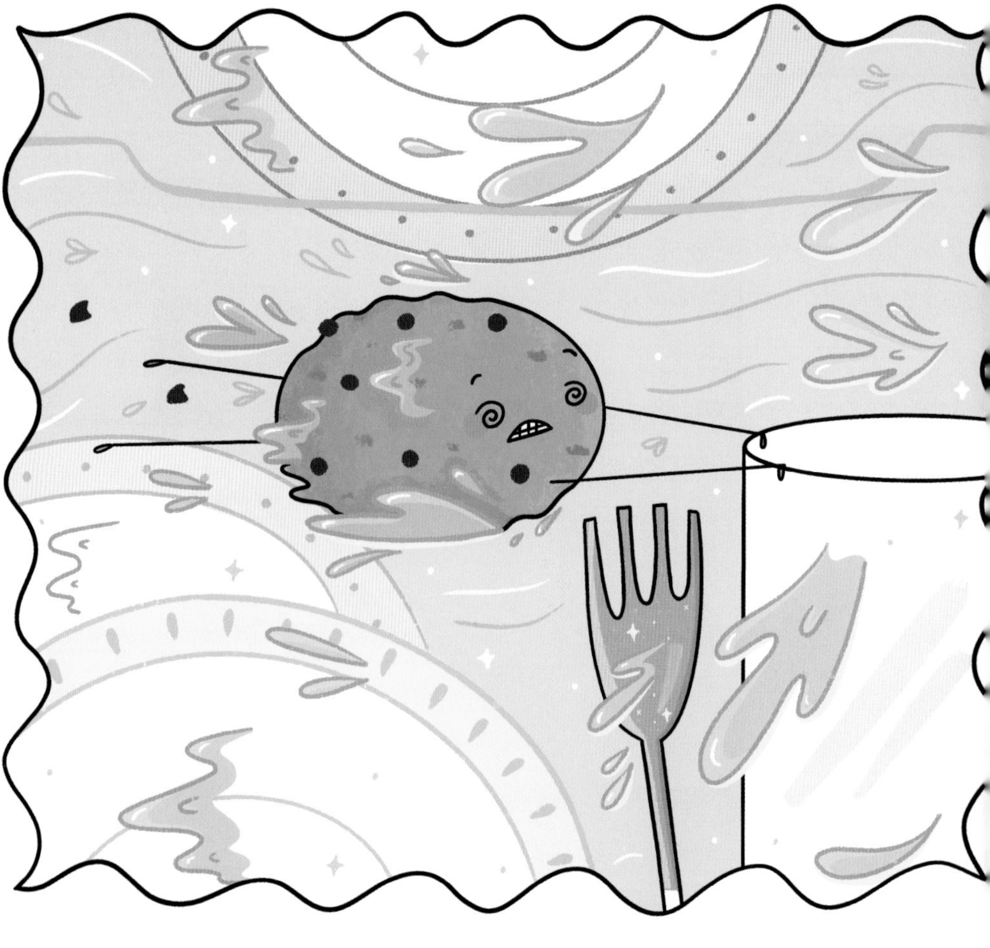

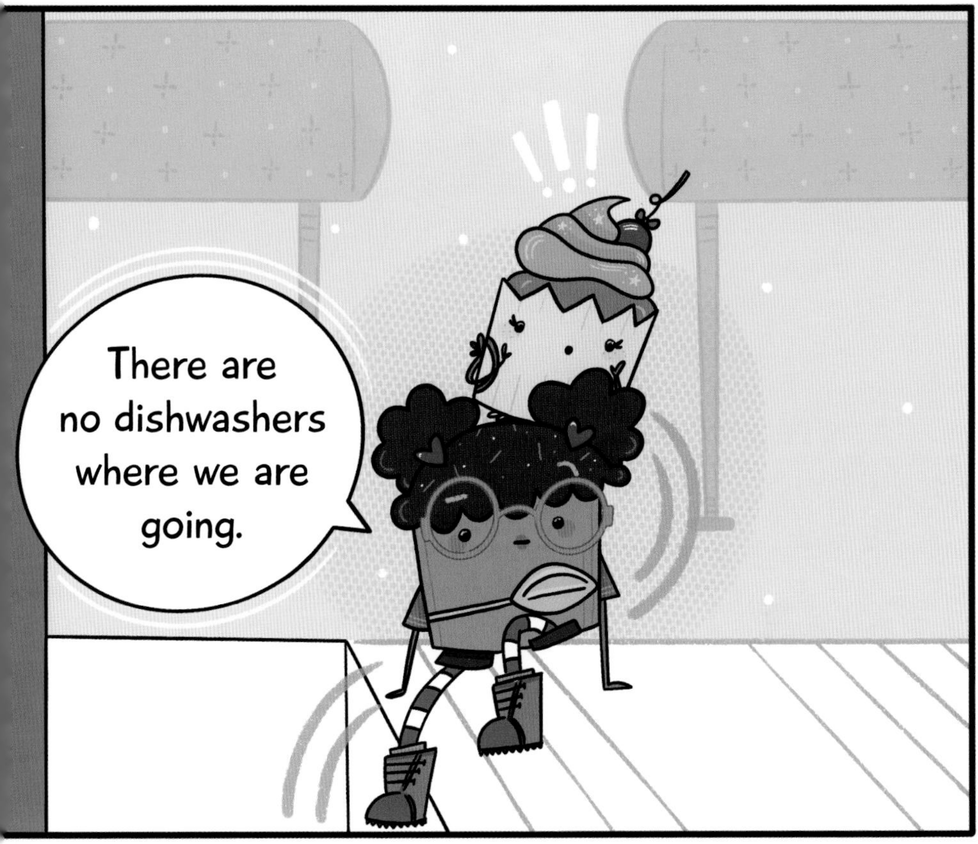
There are no dishwashers where we are going.

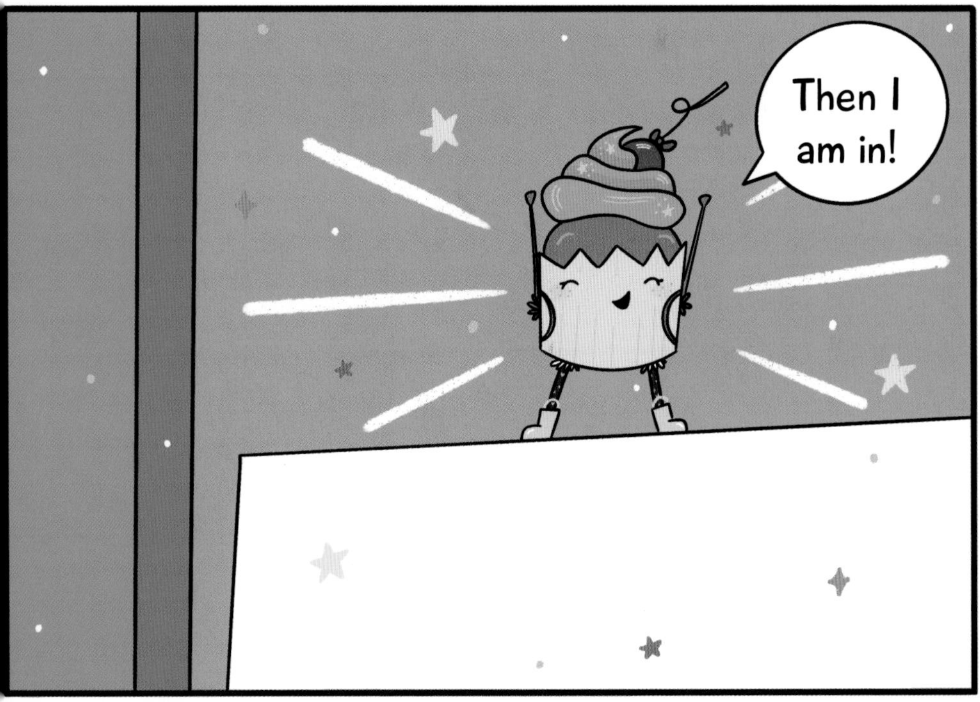
Then I am in!

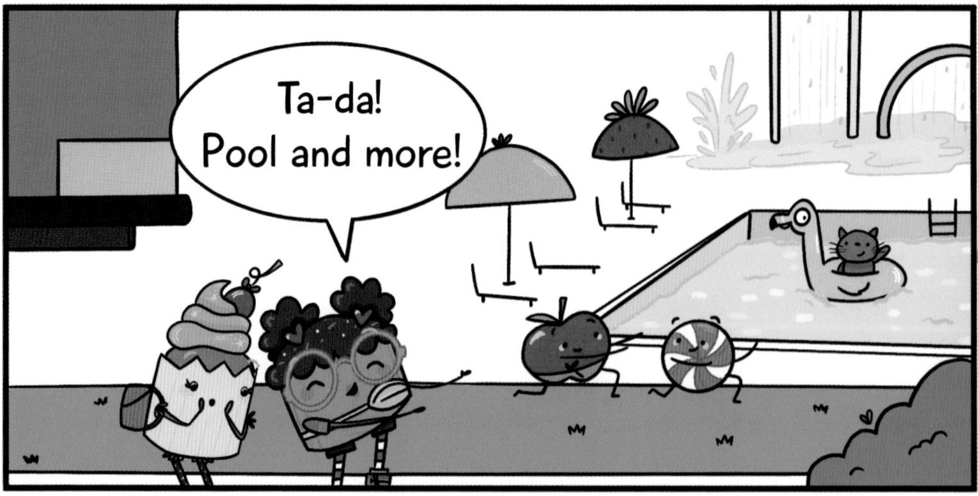
Ta-da! Pool and more!

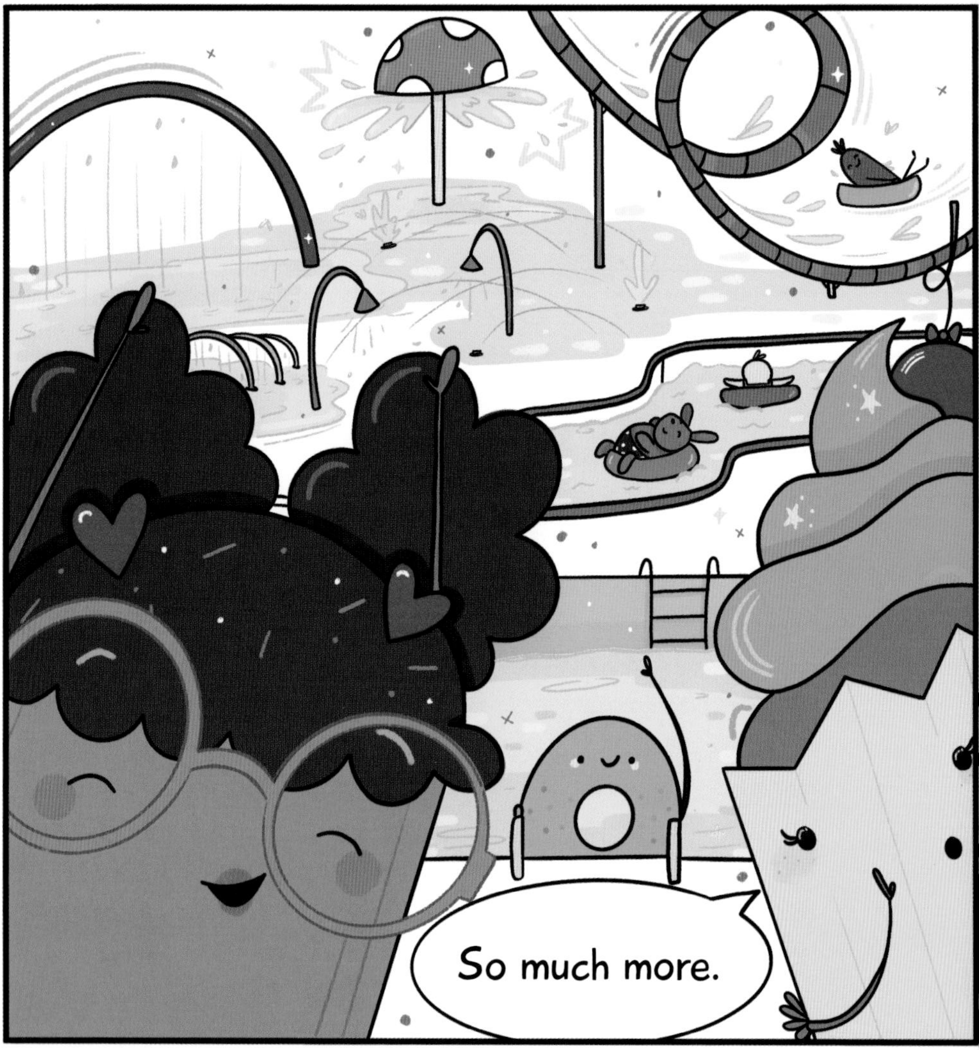
So much more.

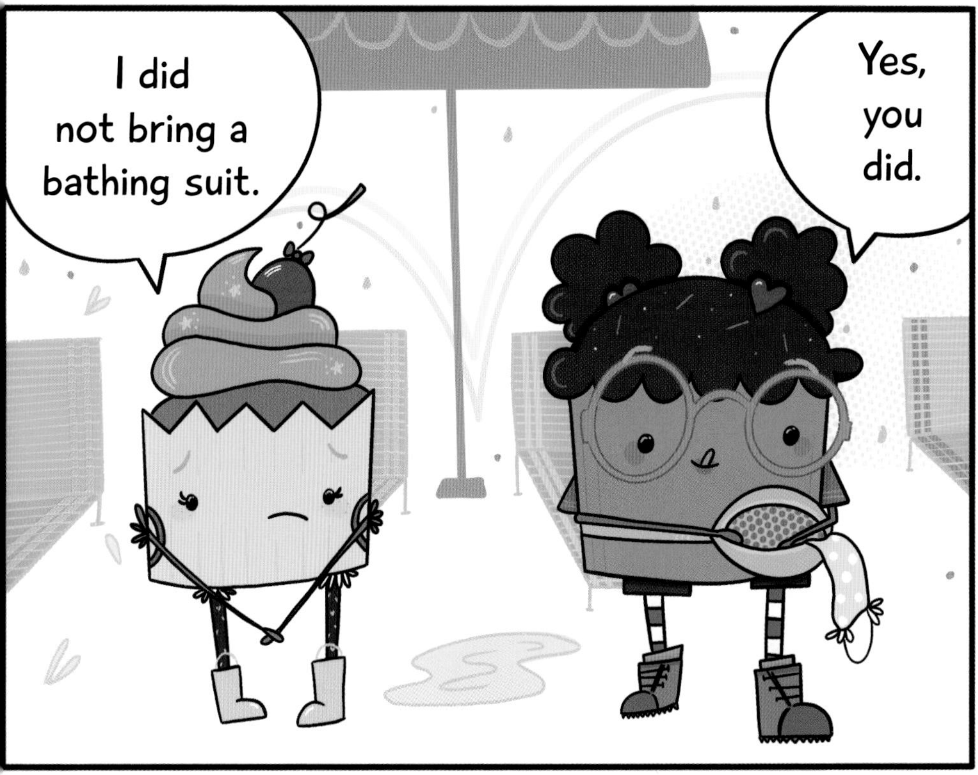
I did not bring a bathing suit.
Yes, you did.

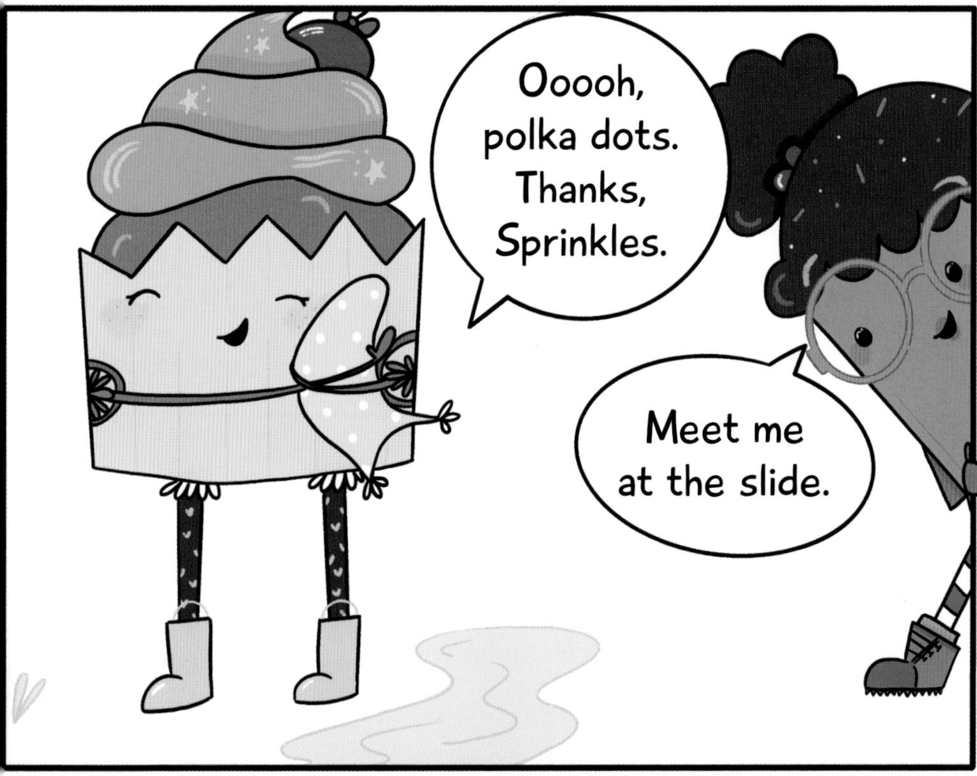
Ooooh, polka dots. Thanks, Sprinkles.
Meet me at the slide.

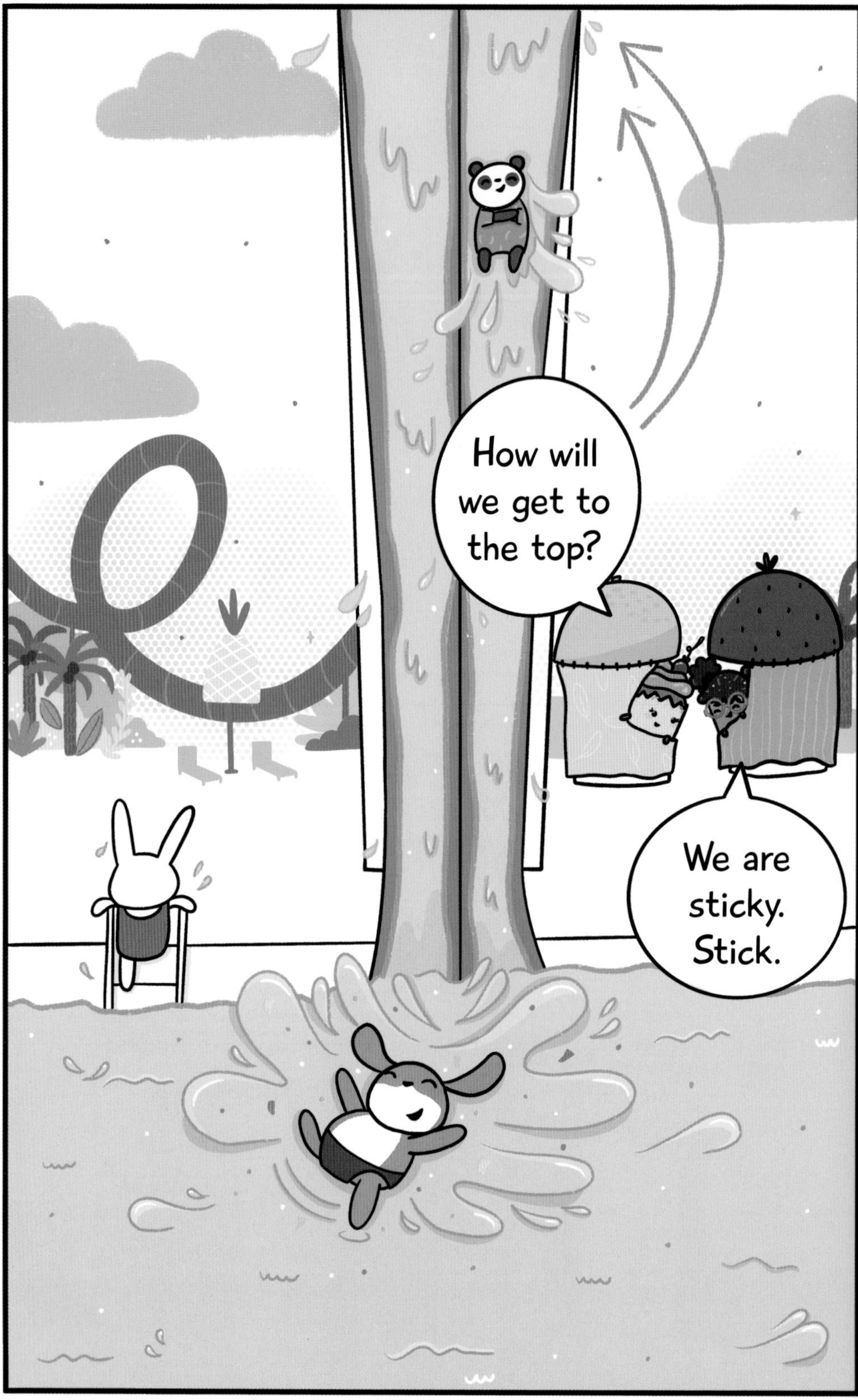
How will we get to the top?
We are sticky. Stick.

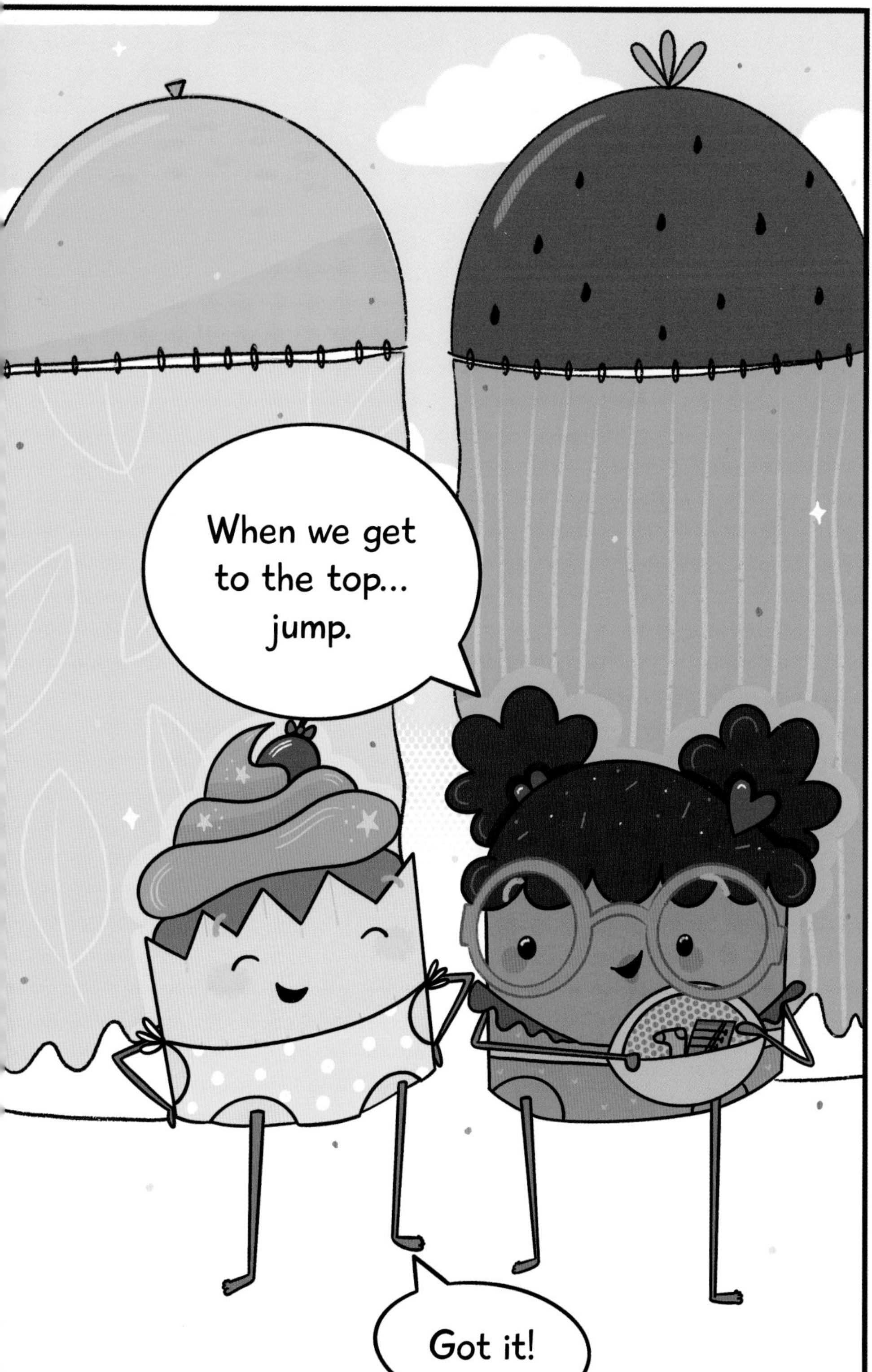
When we get to the top... jump.
Got it!

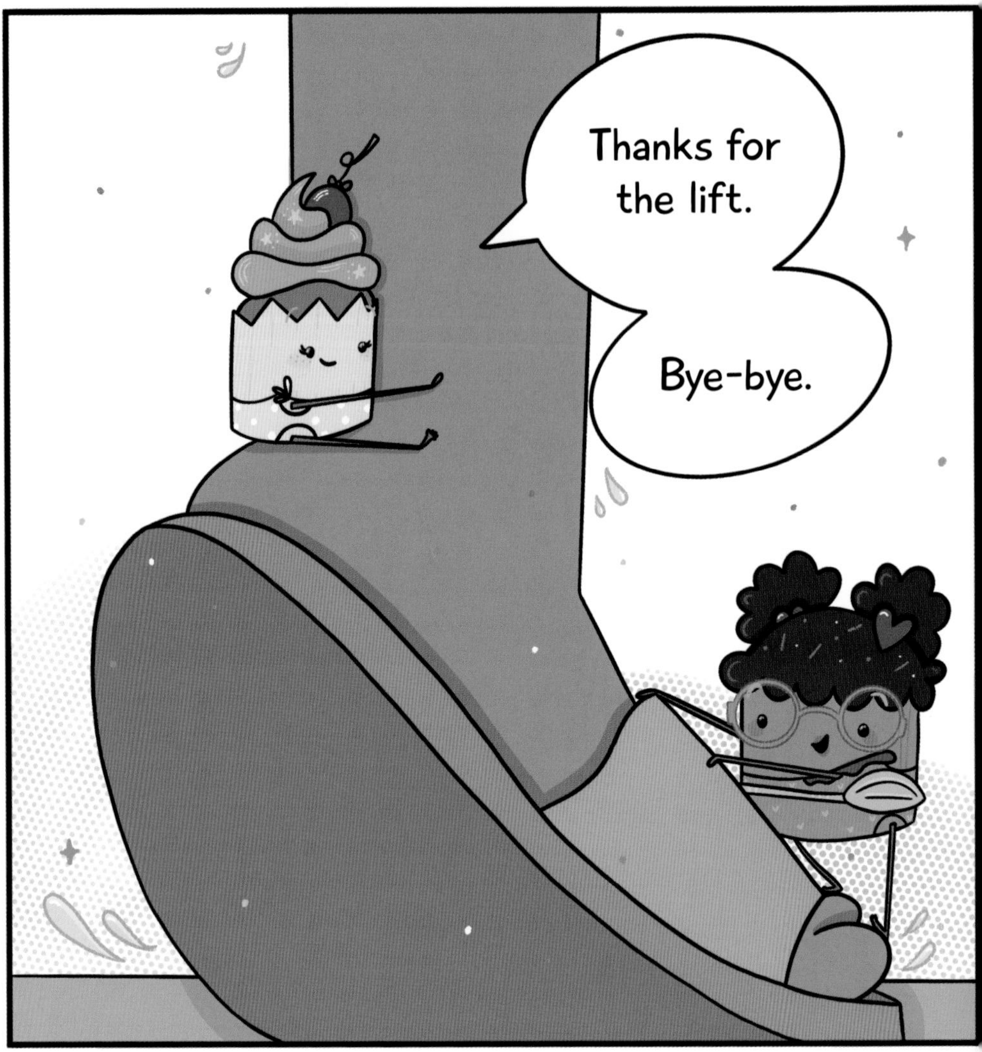
Thanks for the lift.
Bye-bye.

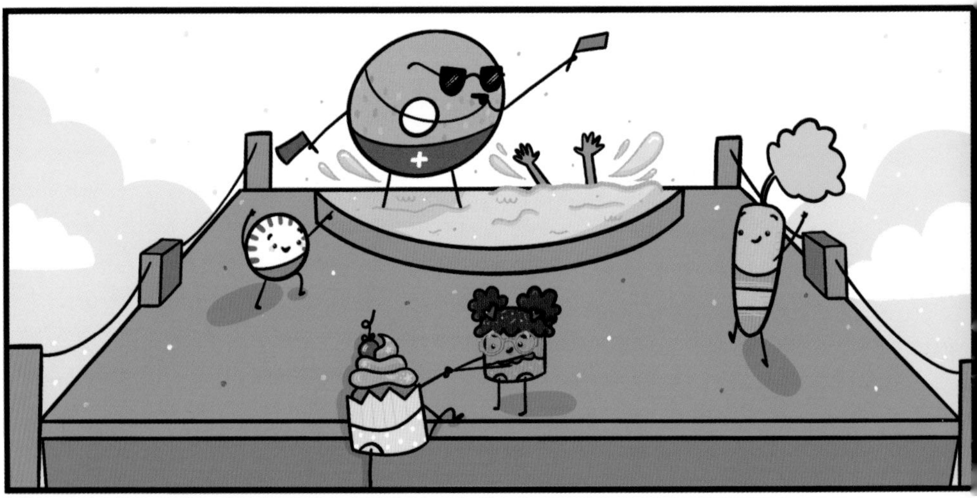

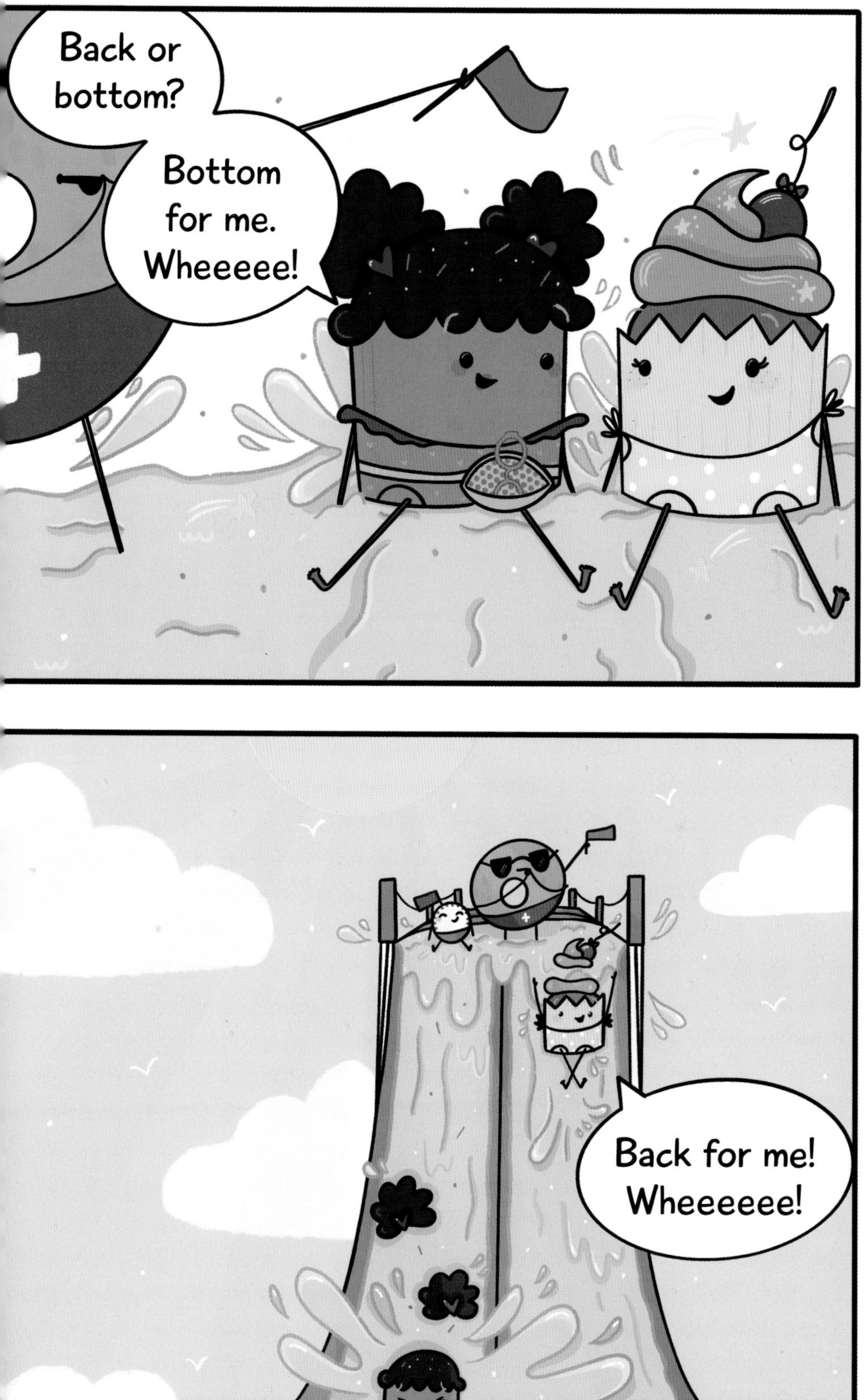
Back or bottom?
Bottom for me. Wheeeee!
Back for me! Wheeeeee!

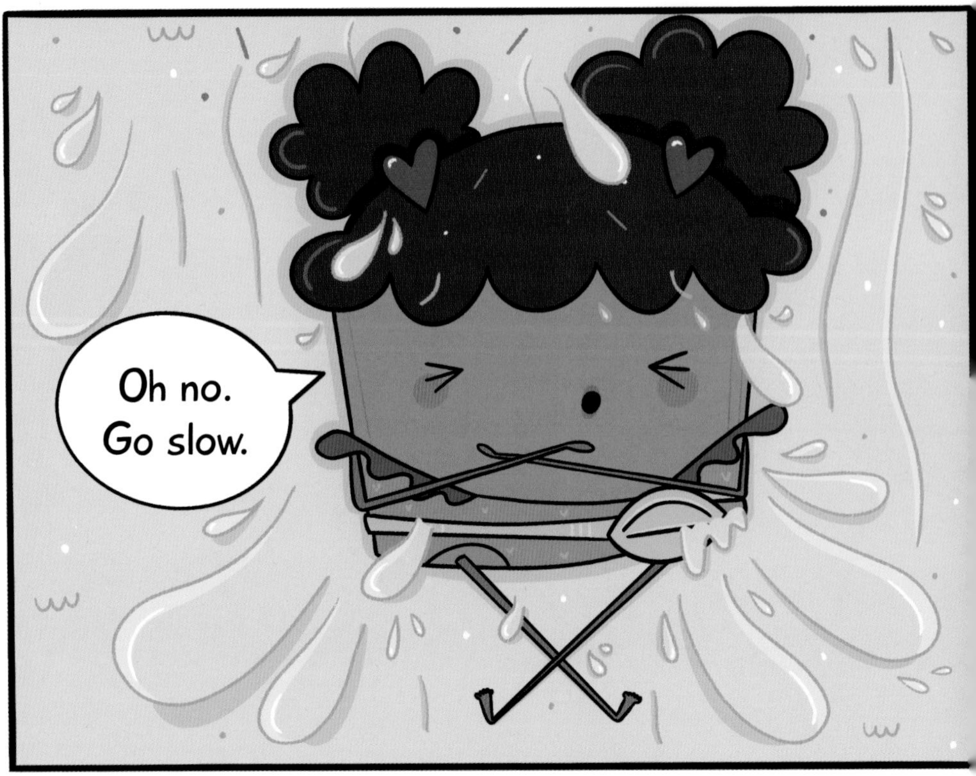
Oh no.
Go slow.

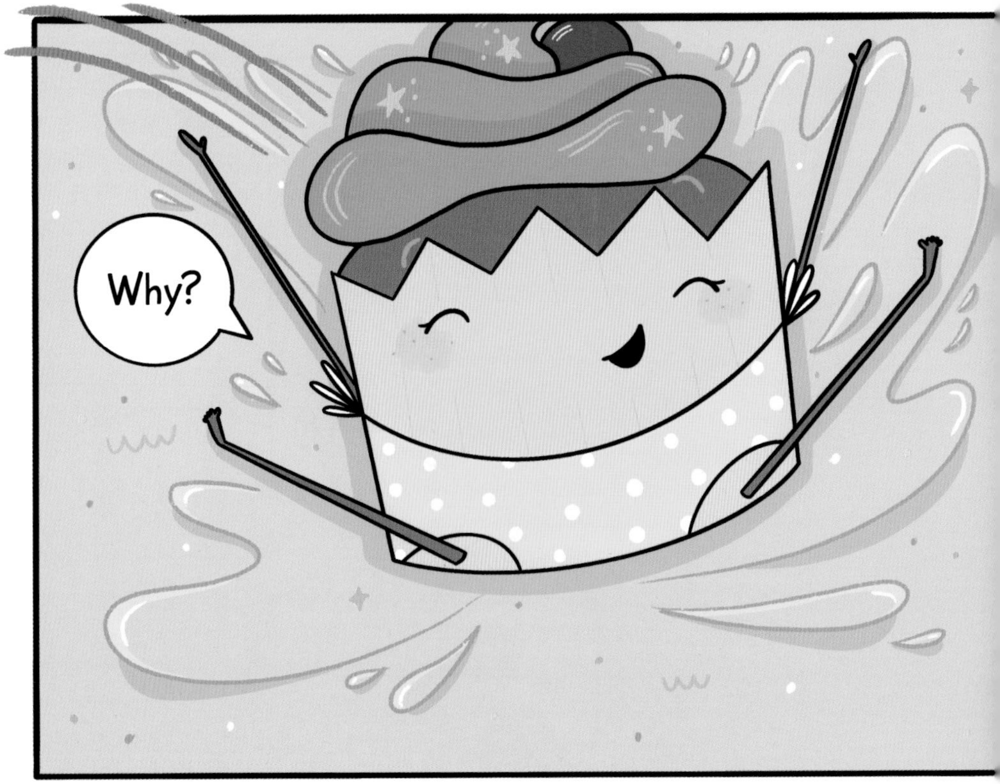
Why?

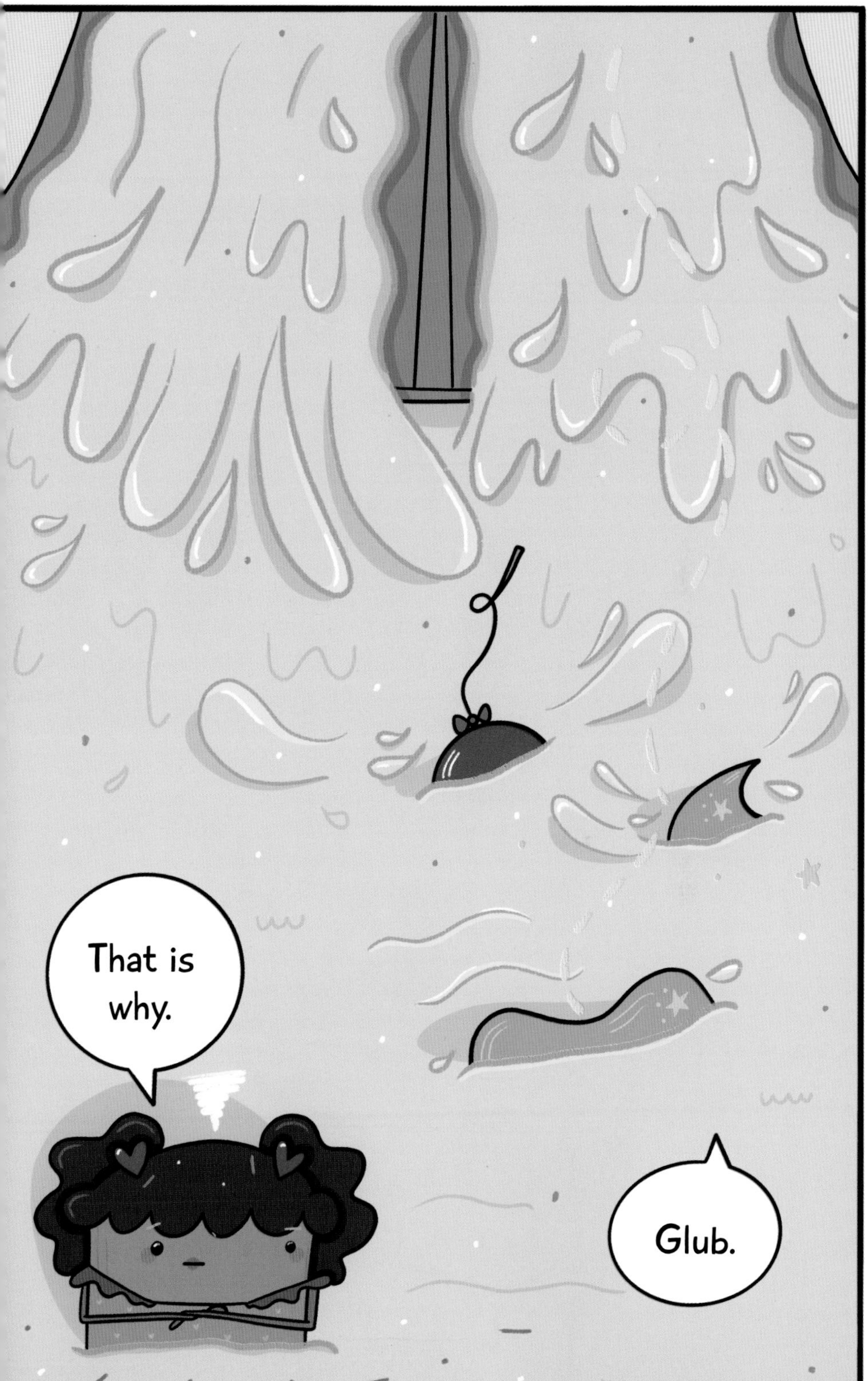
That is why.
Glub.

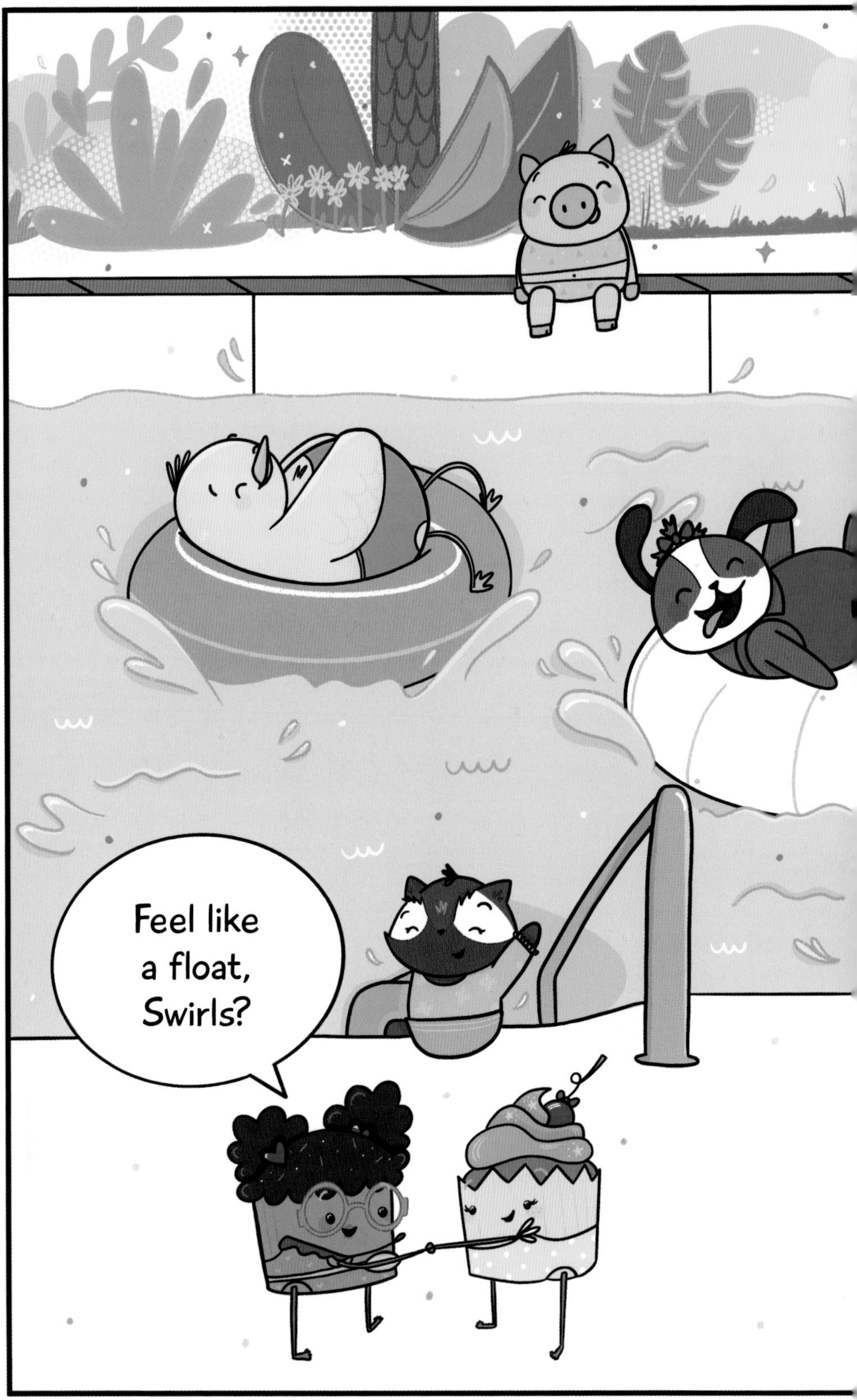
Feel like a float, Swirls?

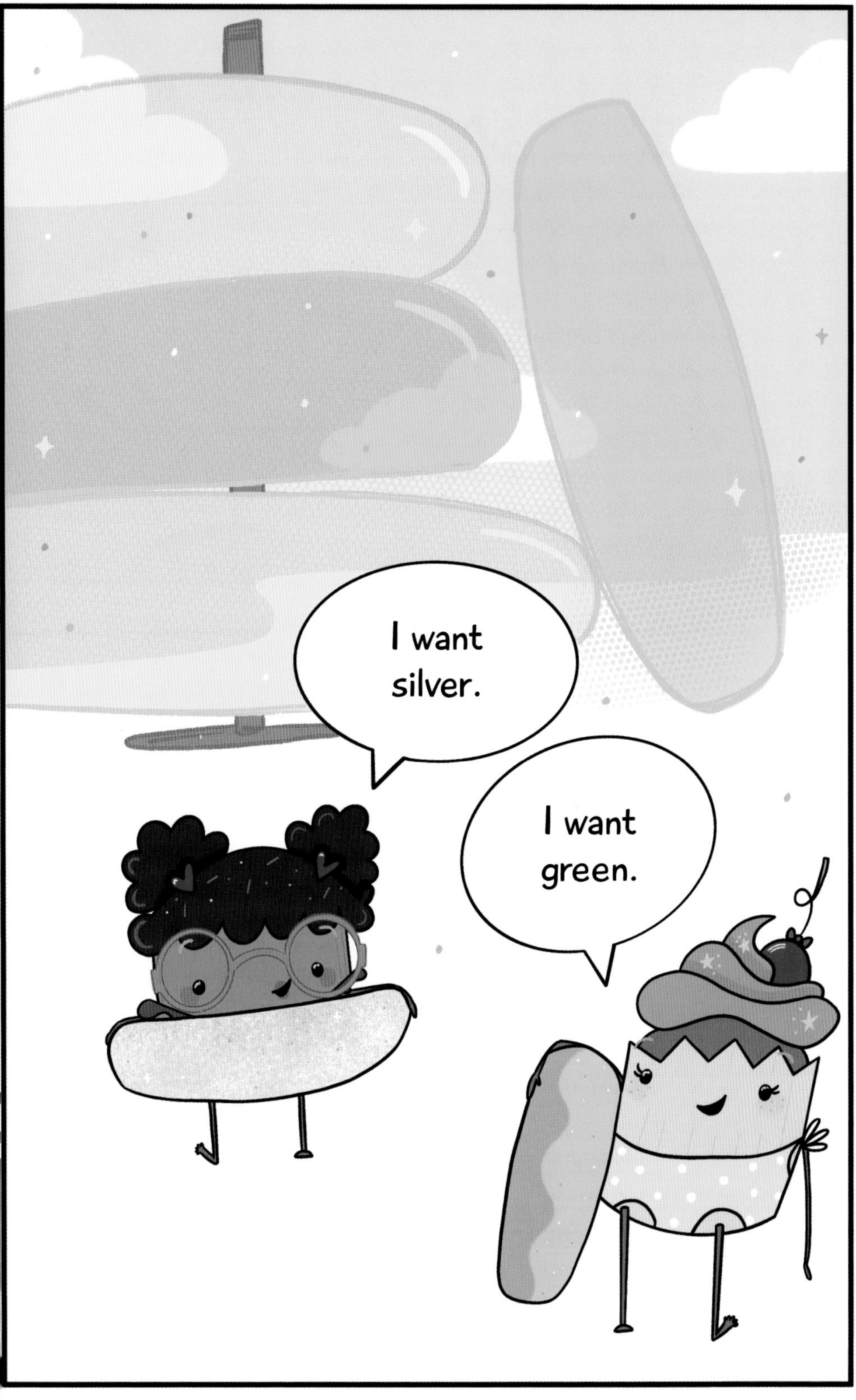
I want silver.
I want green.

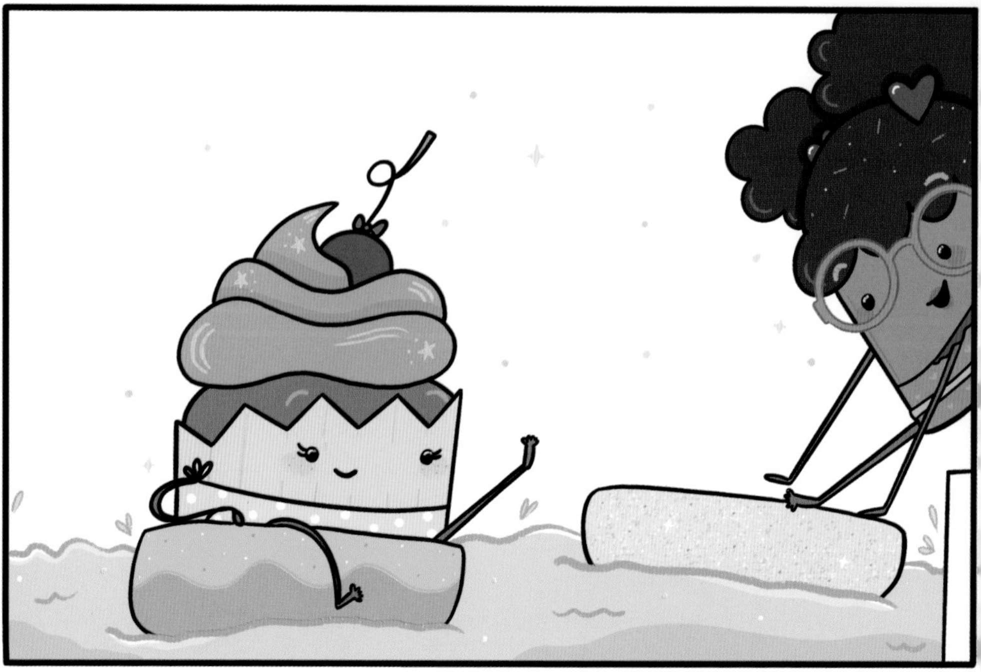

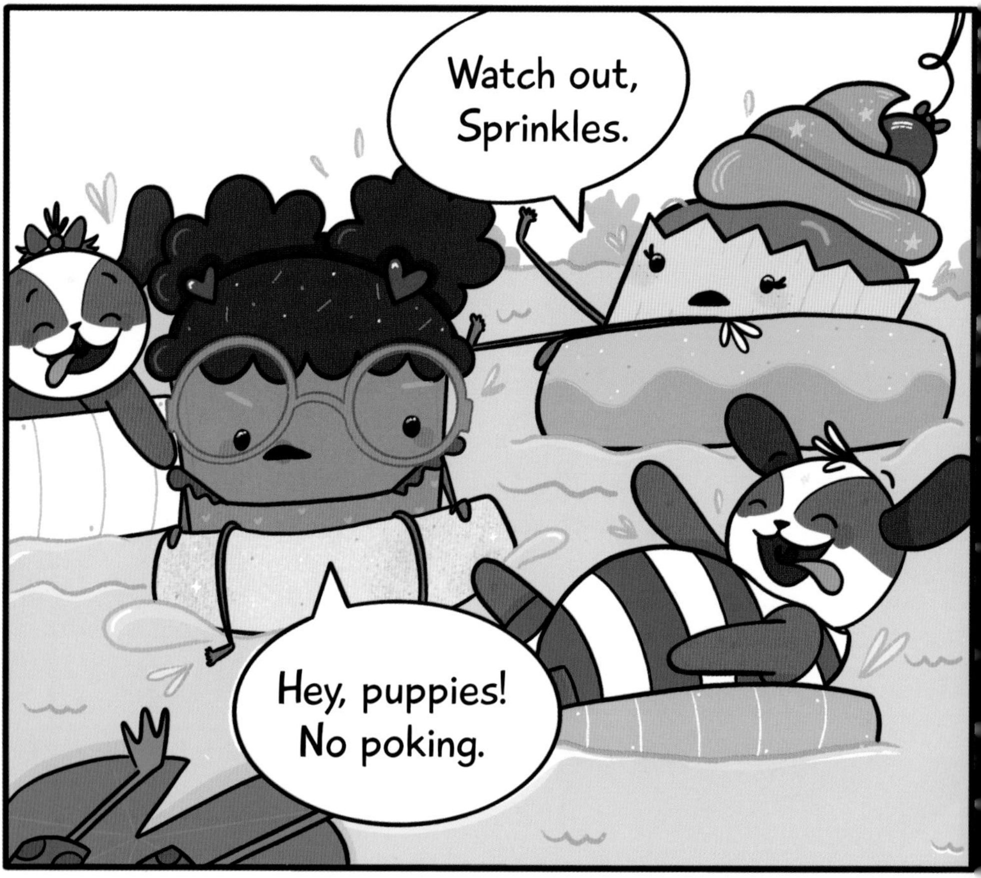
Watch out, Sprinkles.
Hey, puppies! No poking.

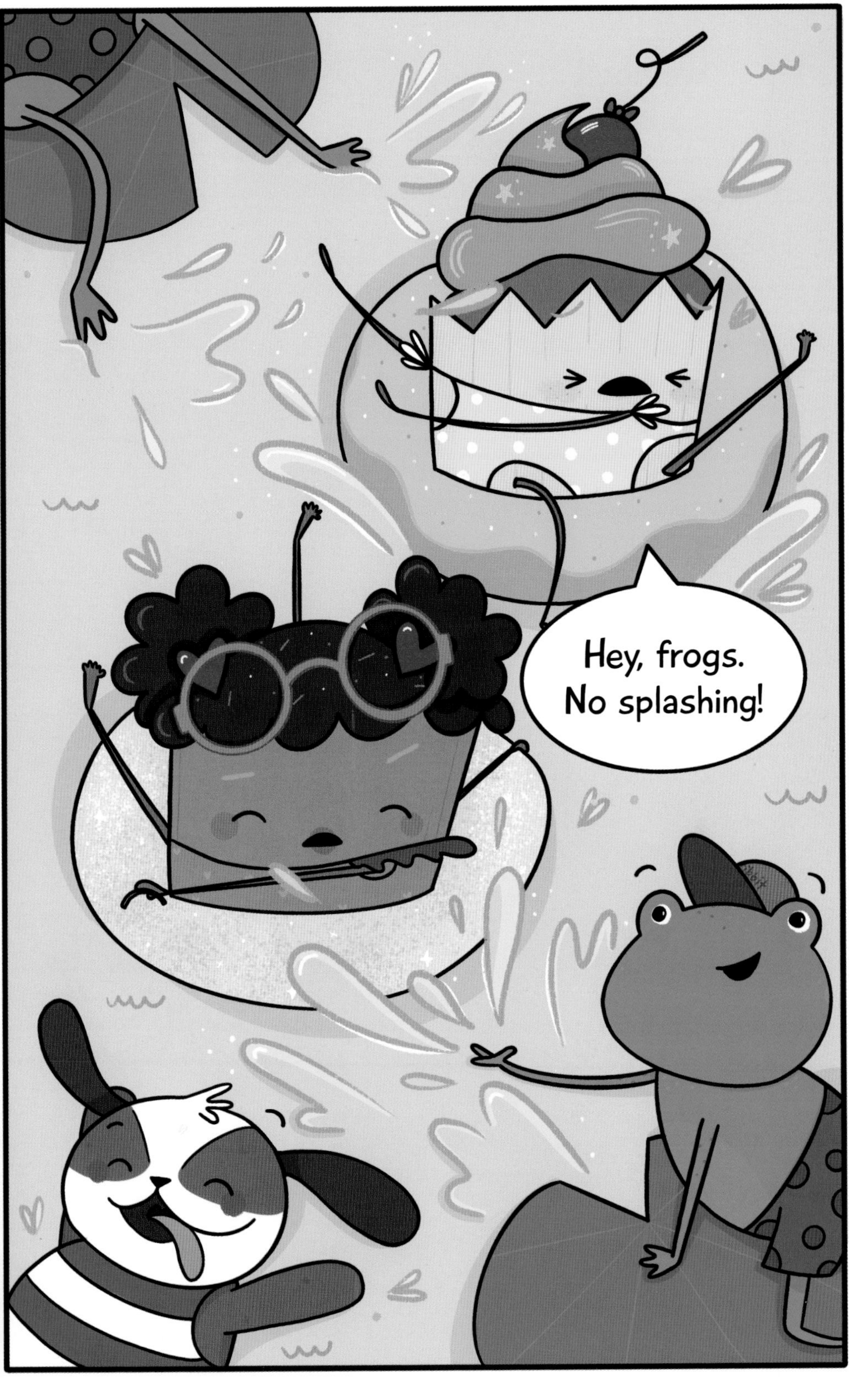
Hey, frogs. No splashing!

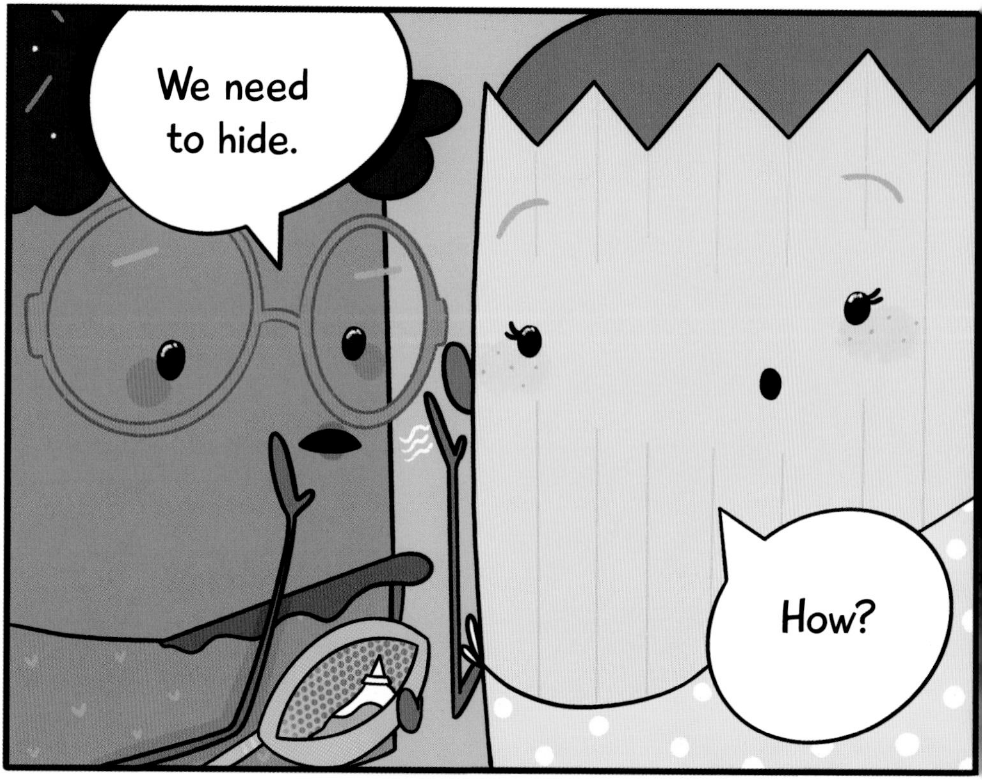
We need to hide.
How?

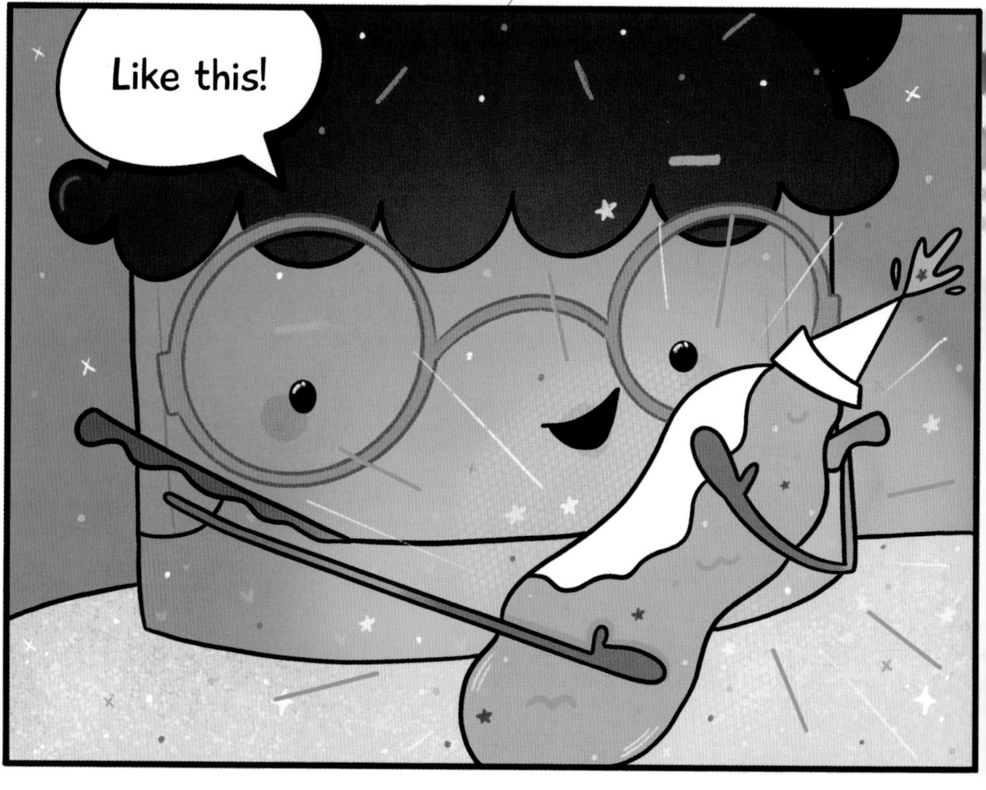
Like this!

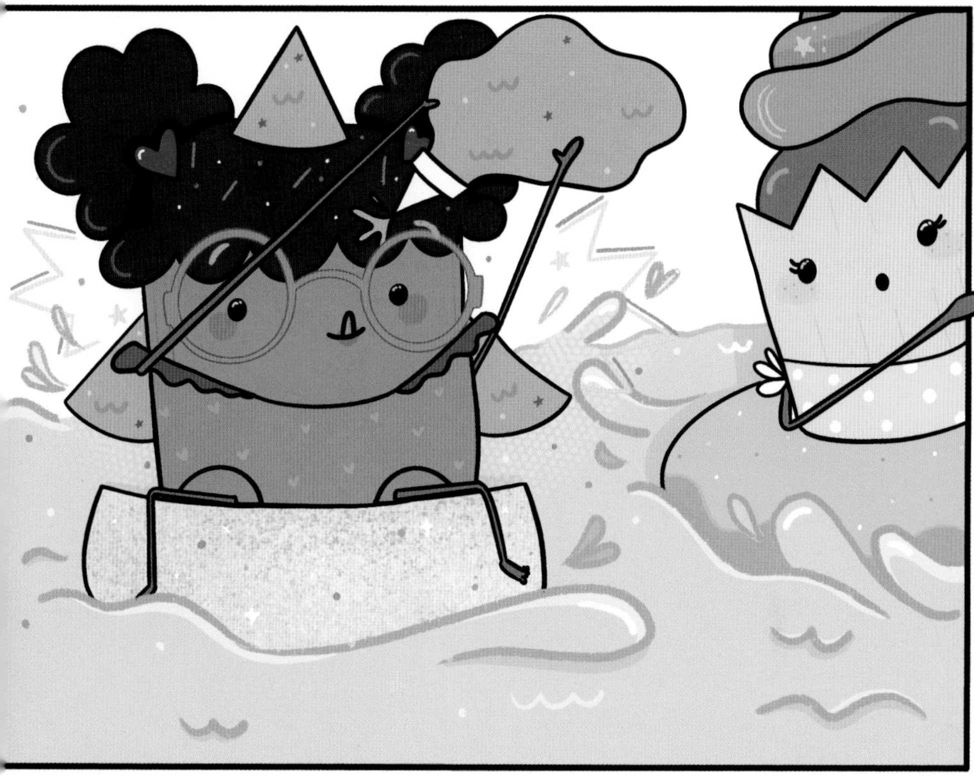

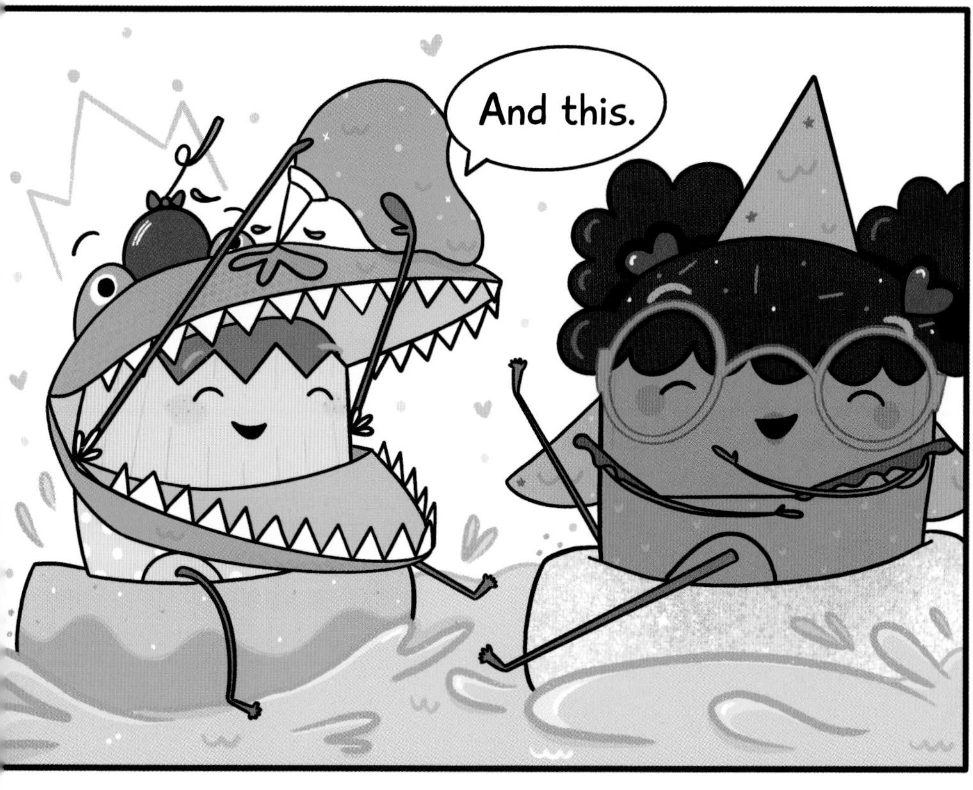
And this.

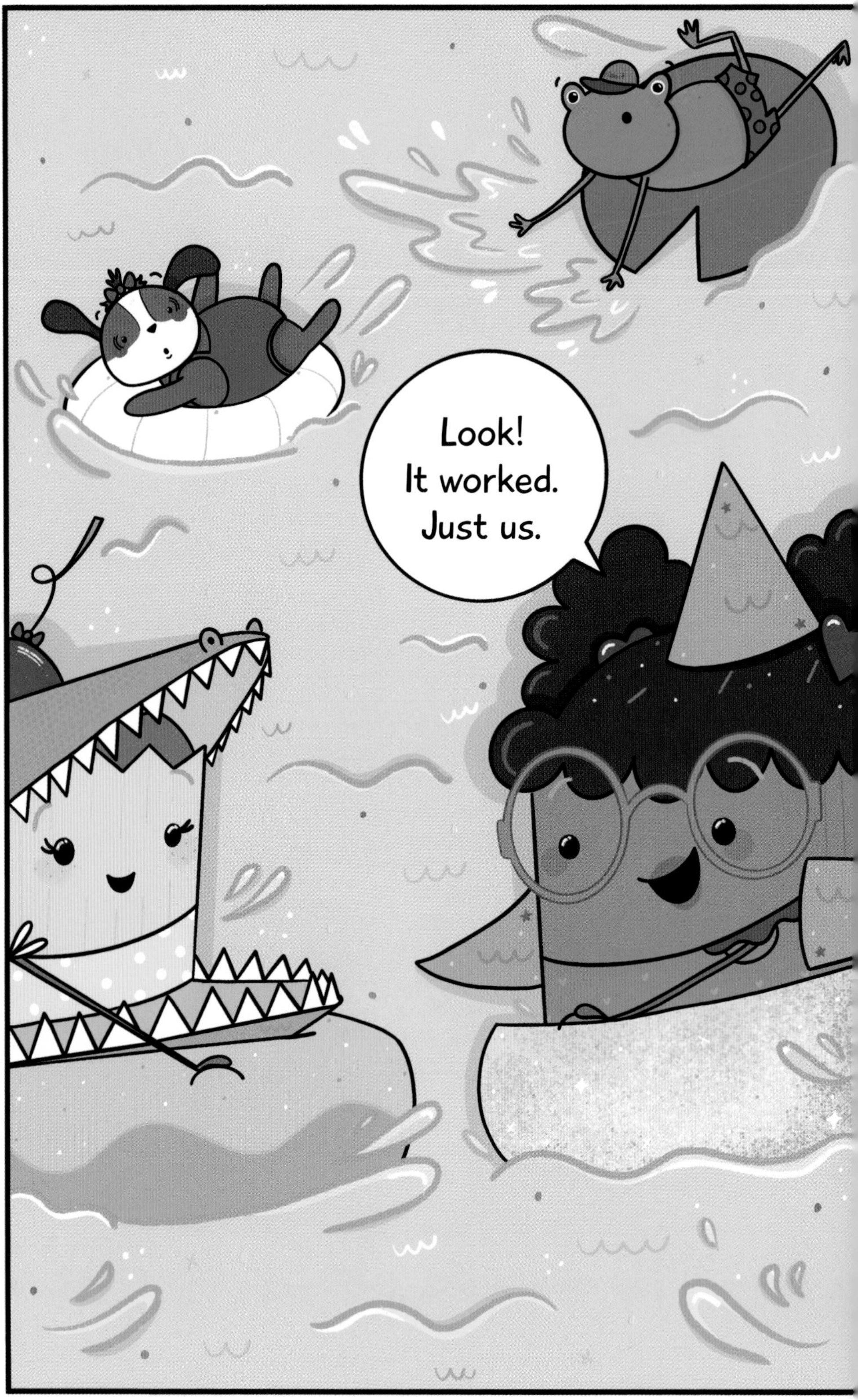
Look! It worked. Just us.

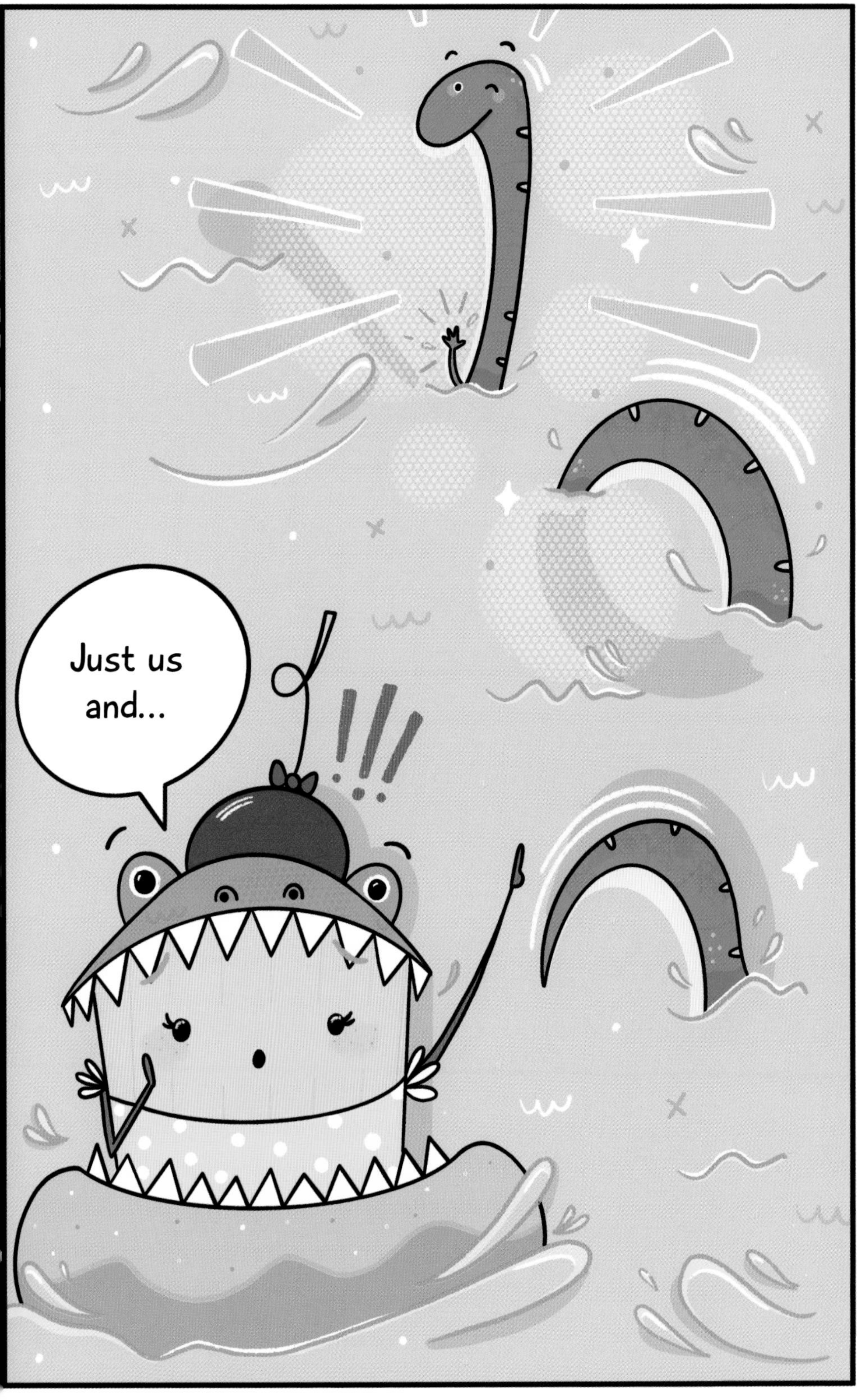
Just us and...
!!!

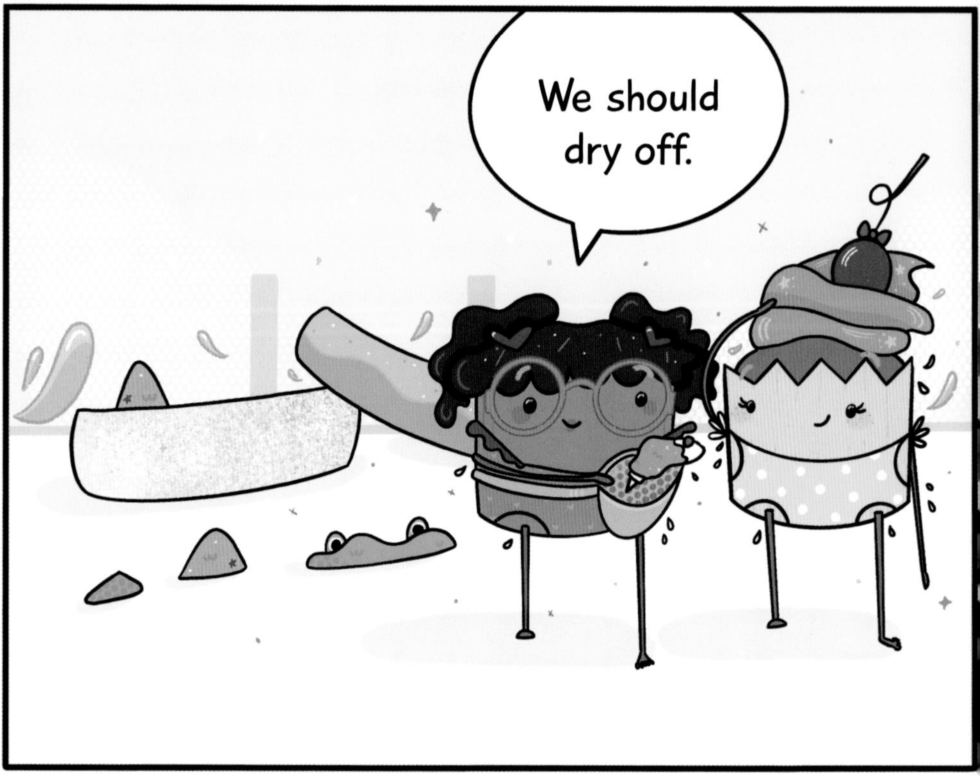
We should dry off.

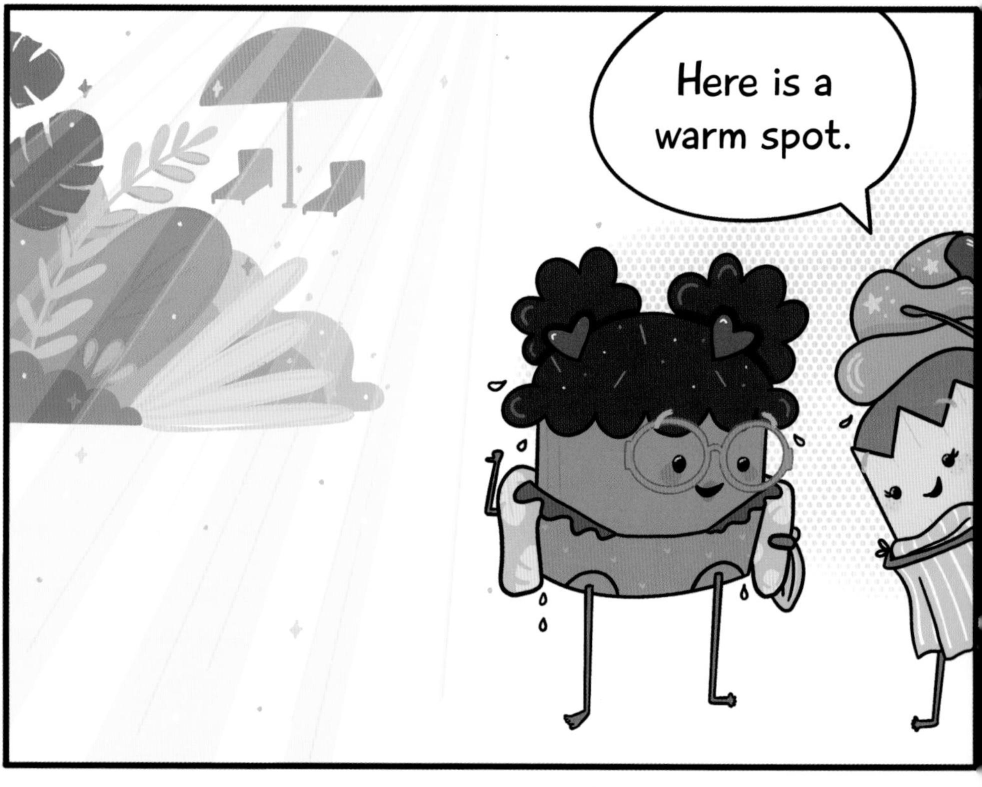
Here is a warm spot.

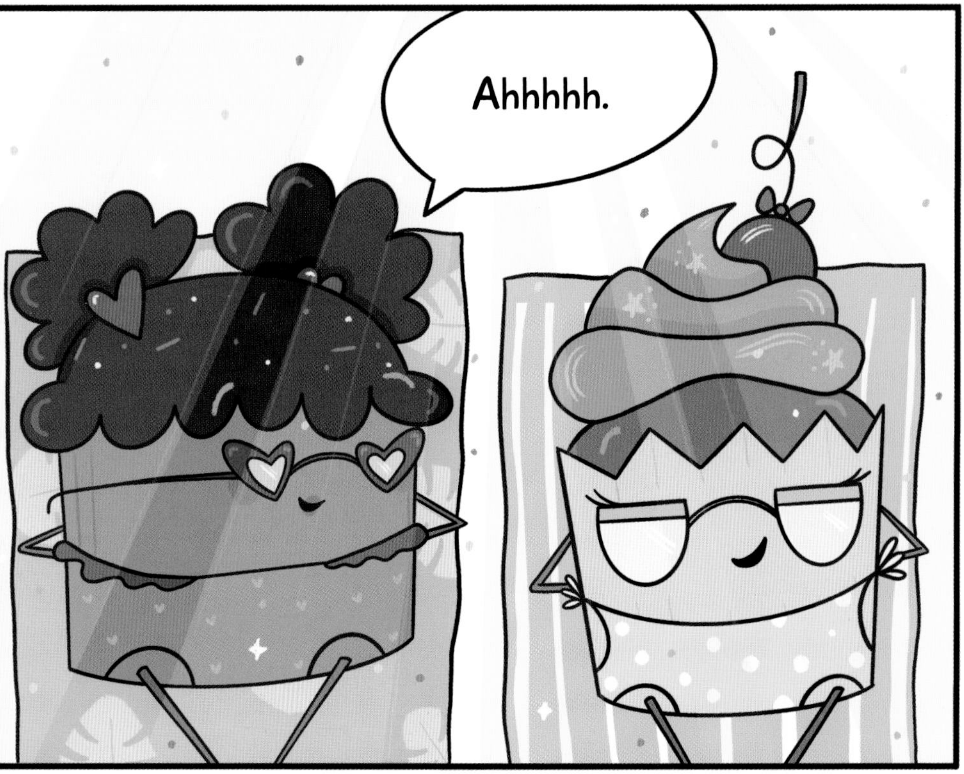
Ahhhhh.

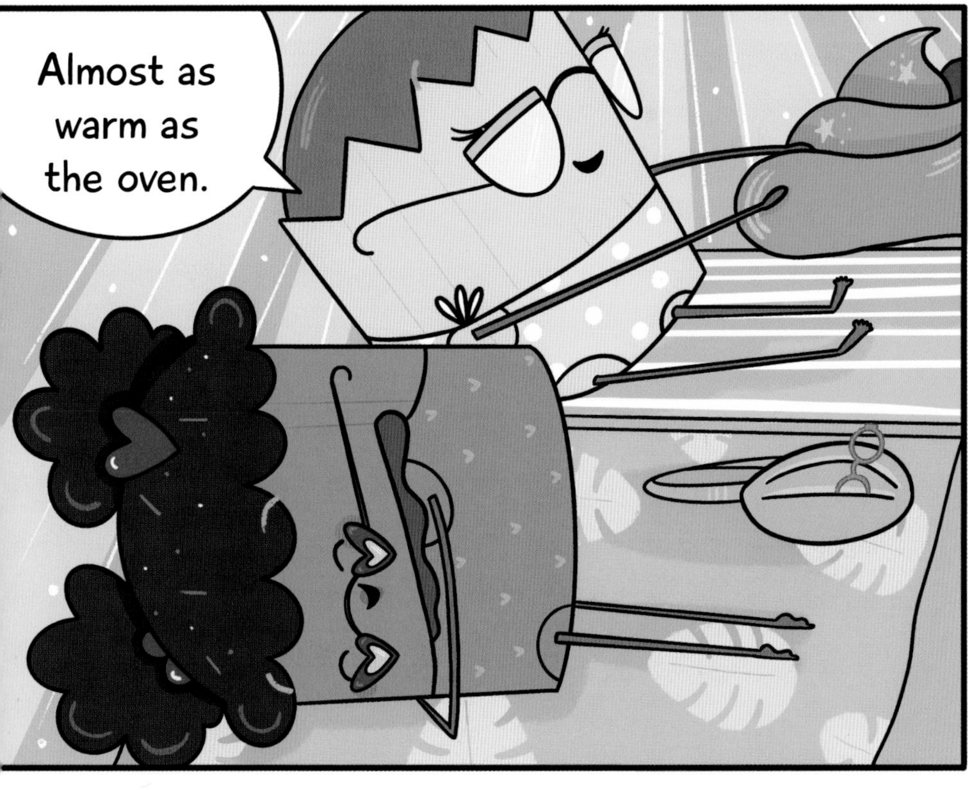
Almost as warm as the oven.

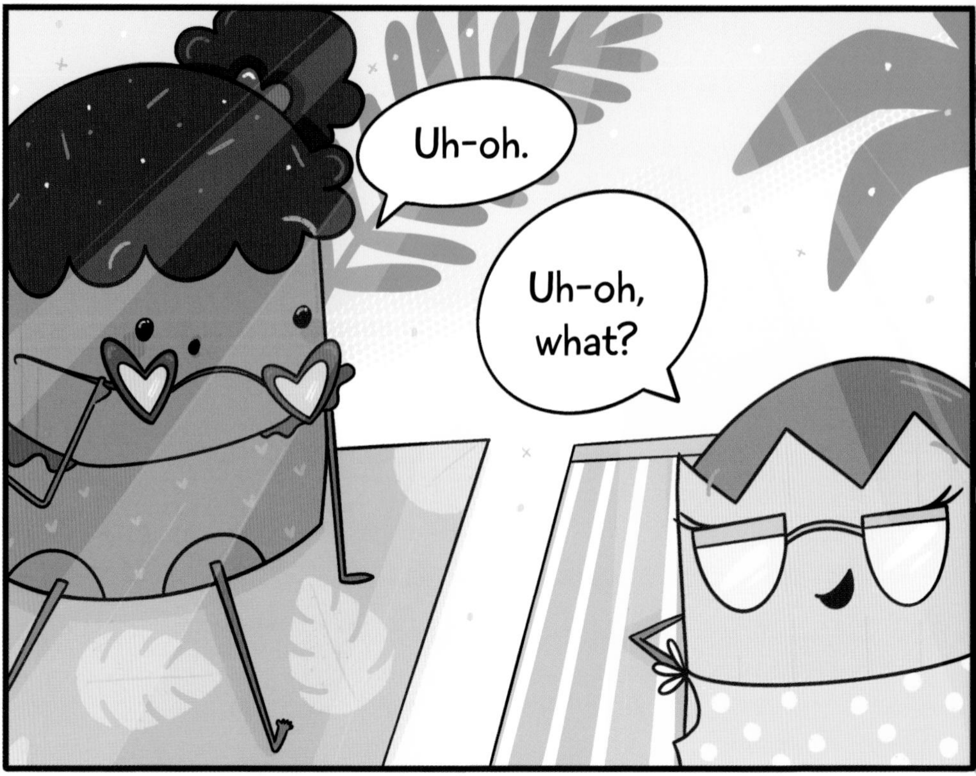
Uh-oh.
Uh-oh, what?

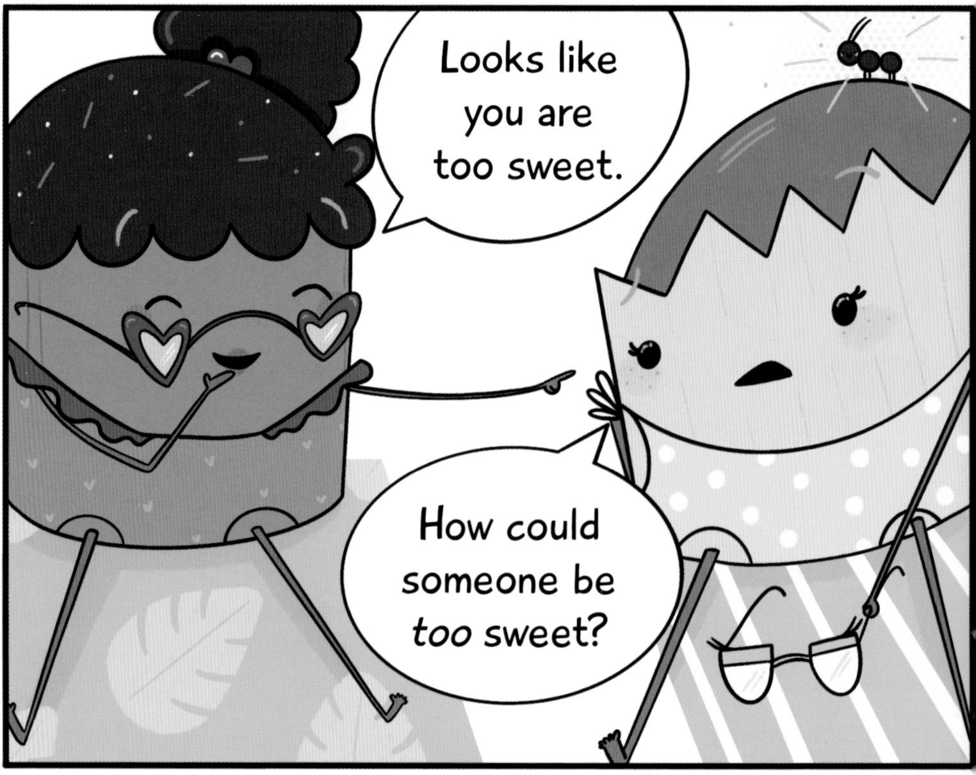
Looks like you are too sweet.
How could someone be *too* sweet?

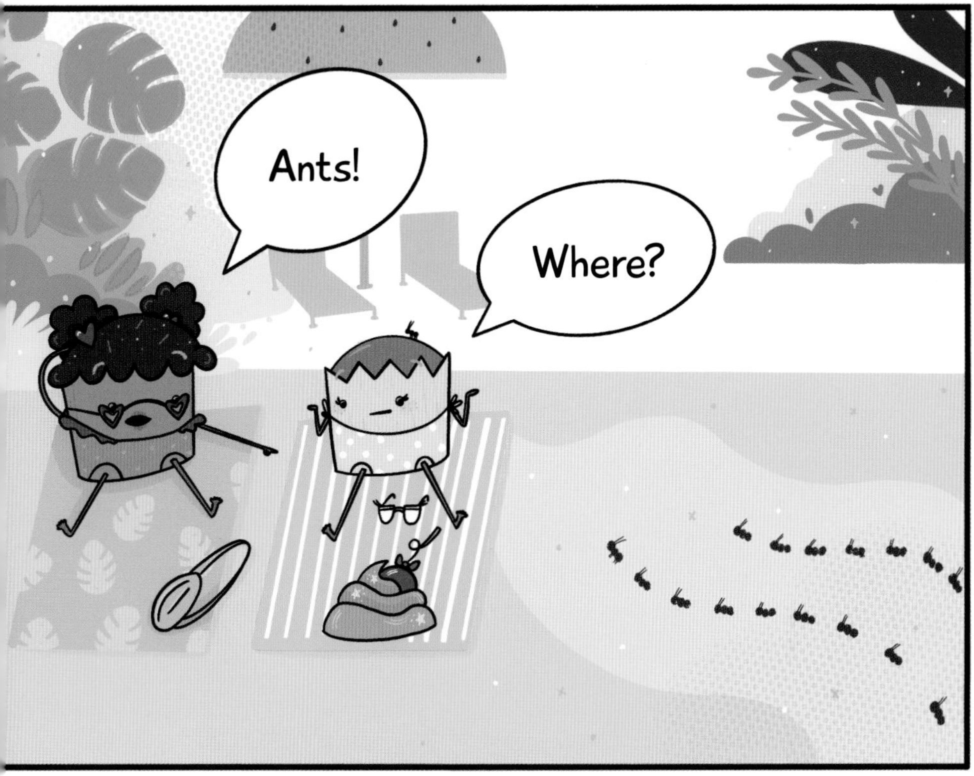
Ants!
Where?

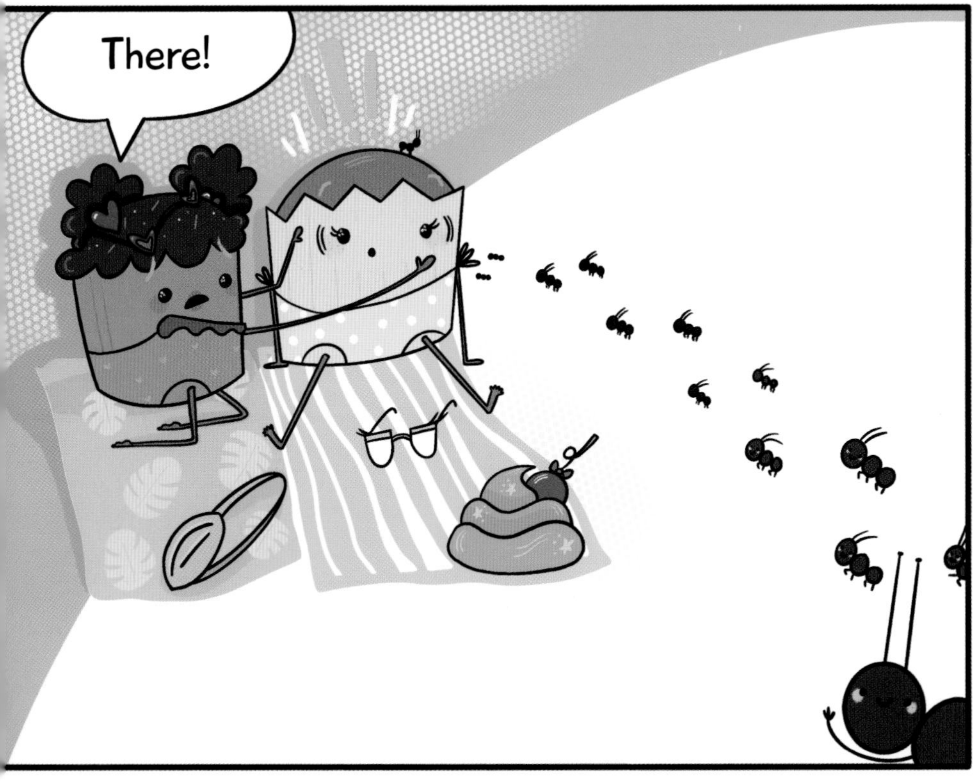
There!

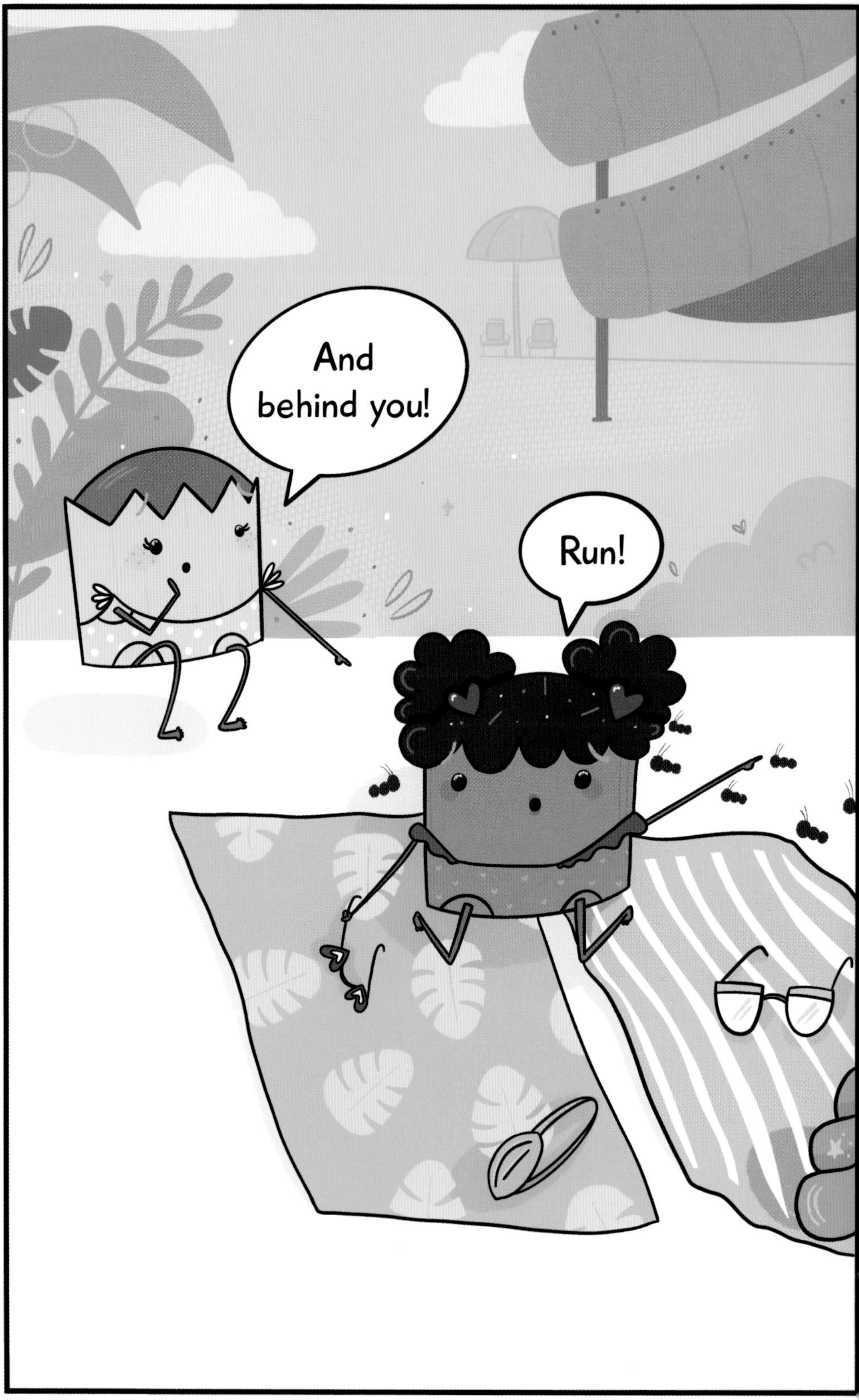
And behind you!
Run!

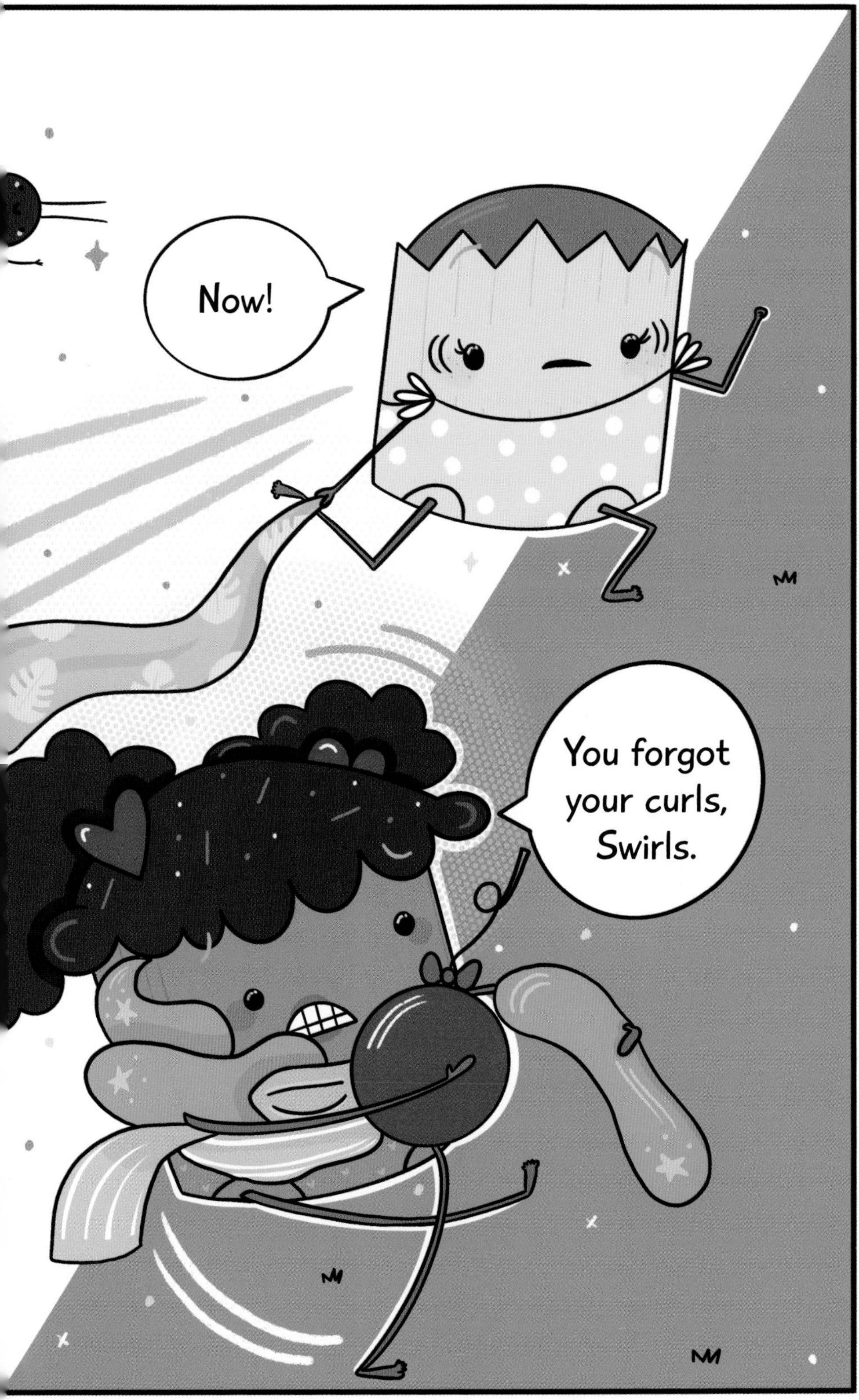
Now!
You forgot your curls, Swirls.

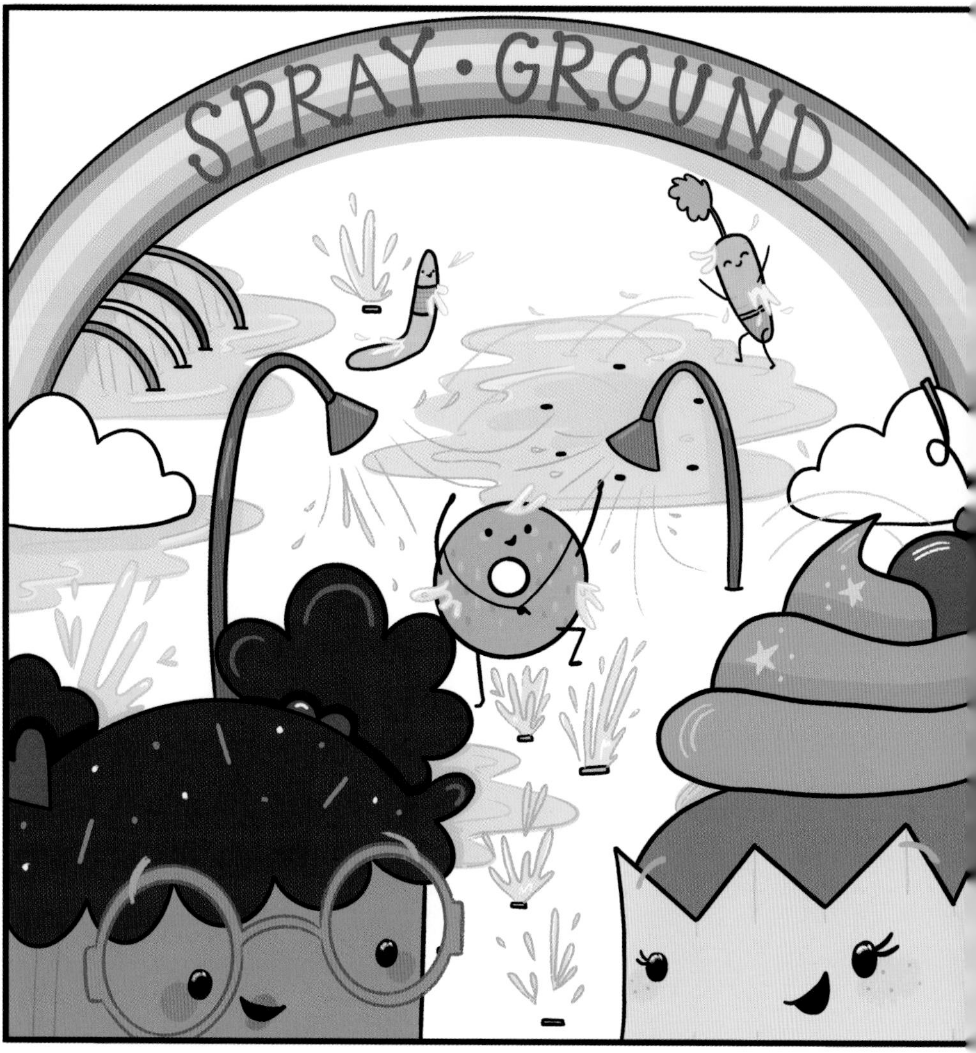
SPRAY • GROUND

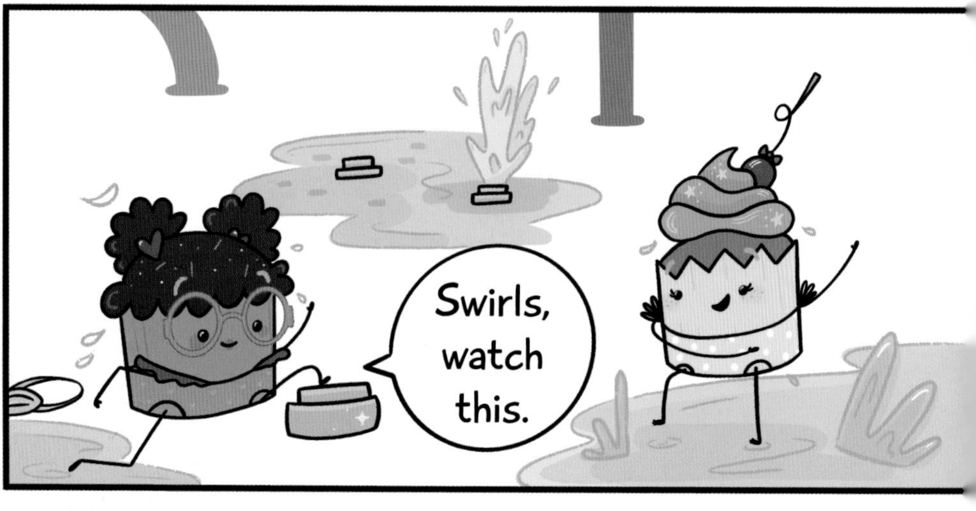
Swirls, watch this.

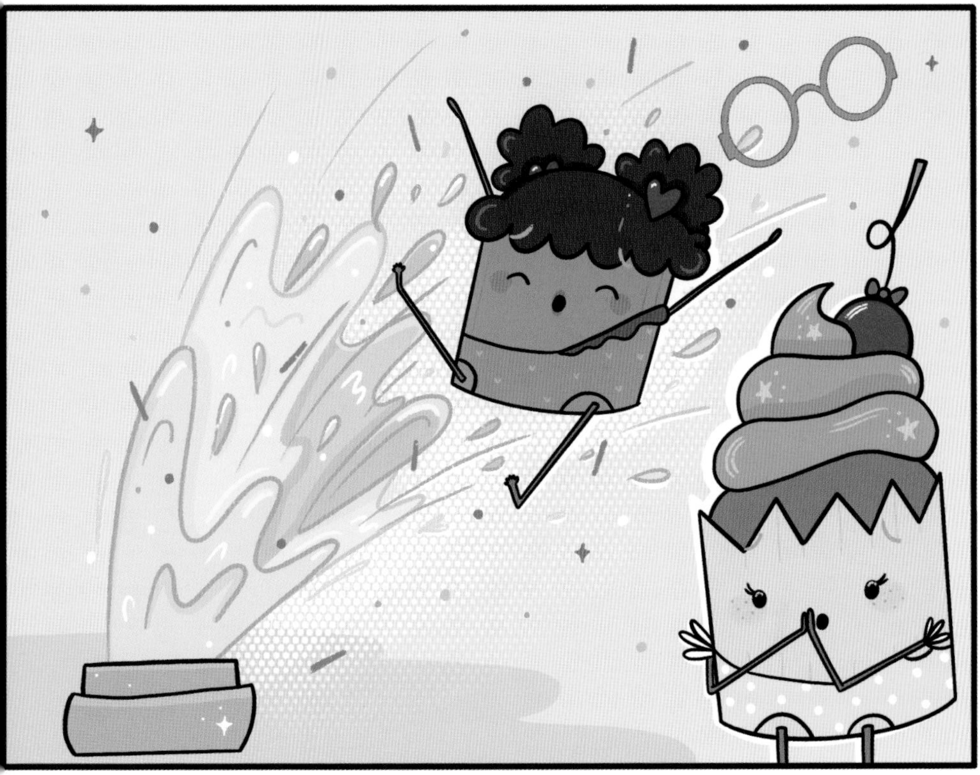

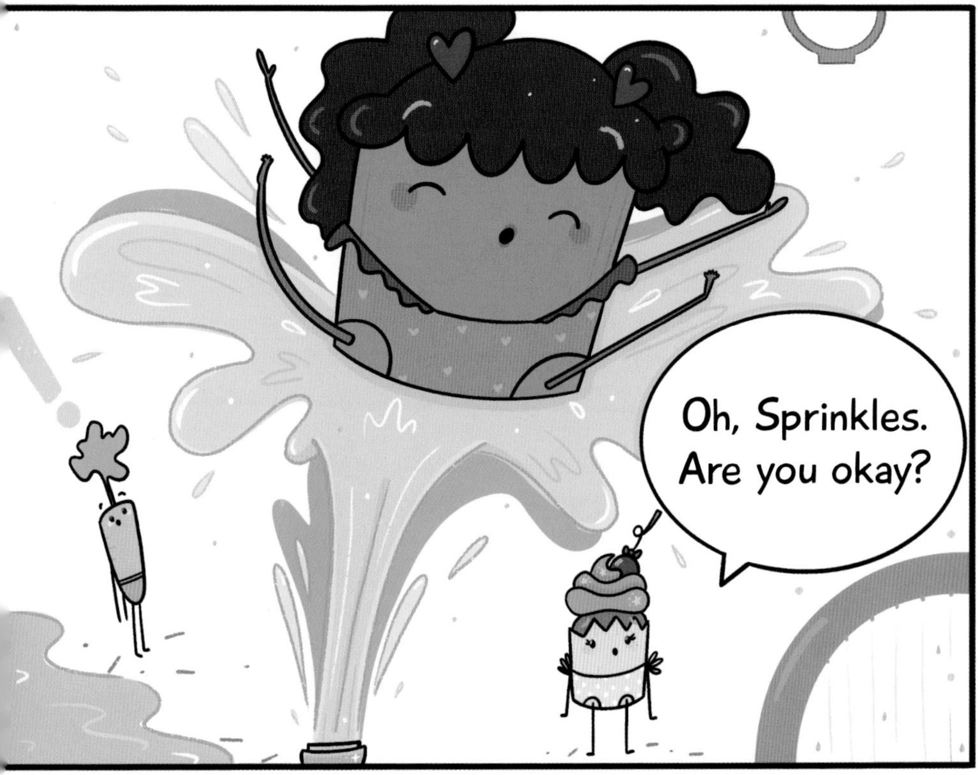
Oh, Sprinkles. Are you okay?

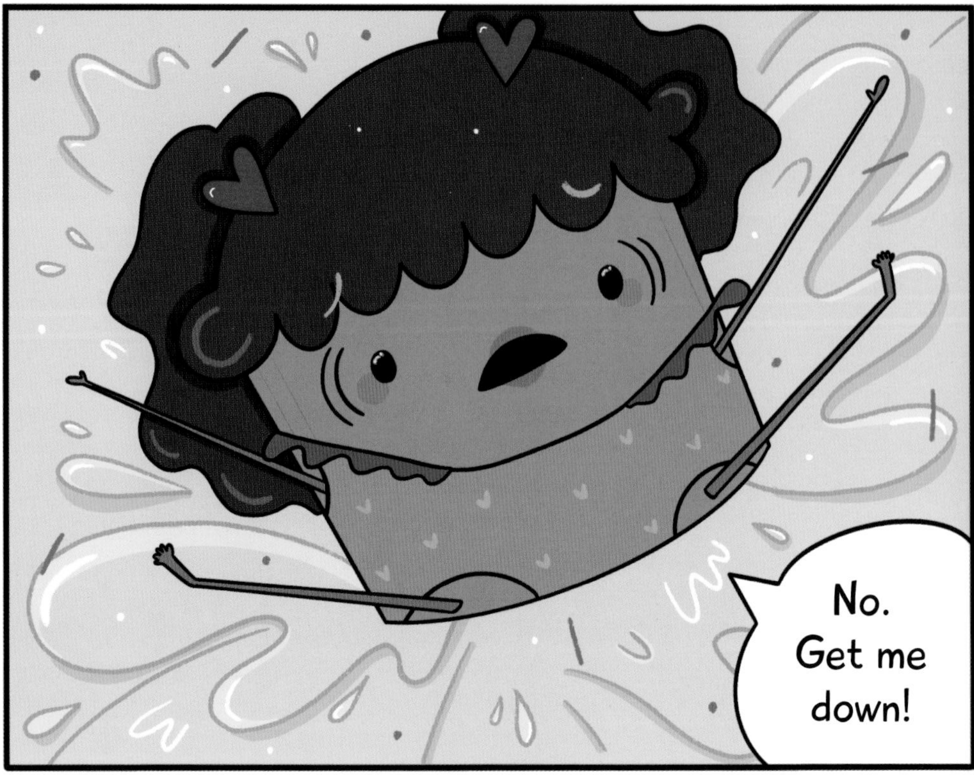
No.
Get me
down!

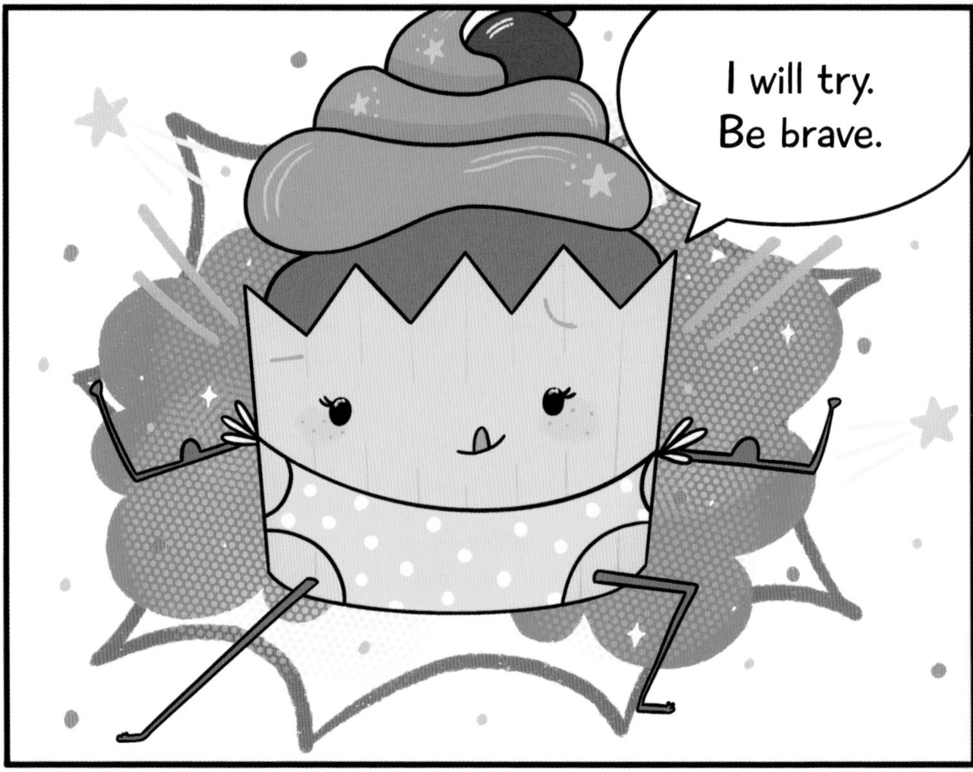
I will try.
Be brave.

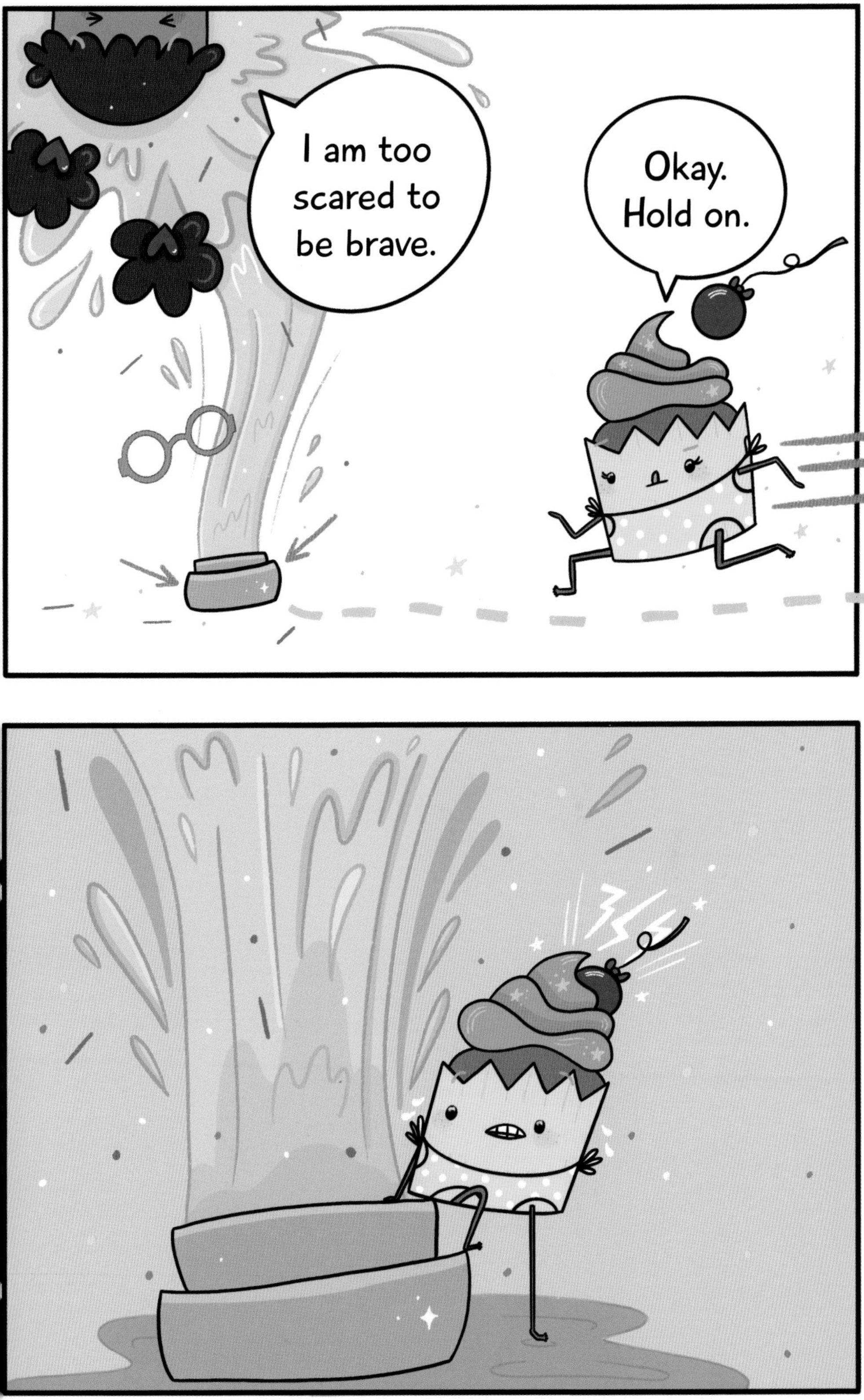
I am too scared to be brave.
Okay. Hold on.

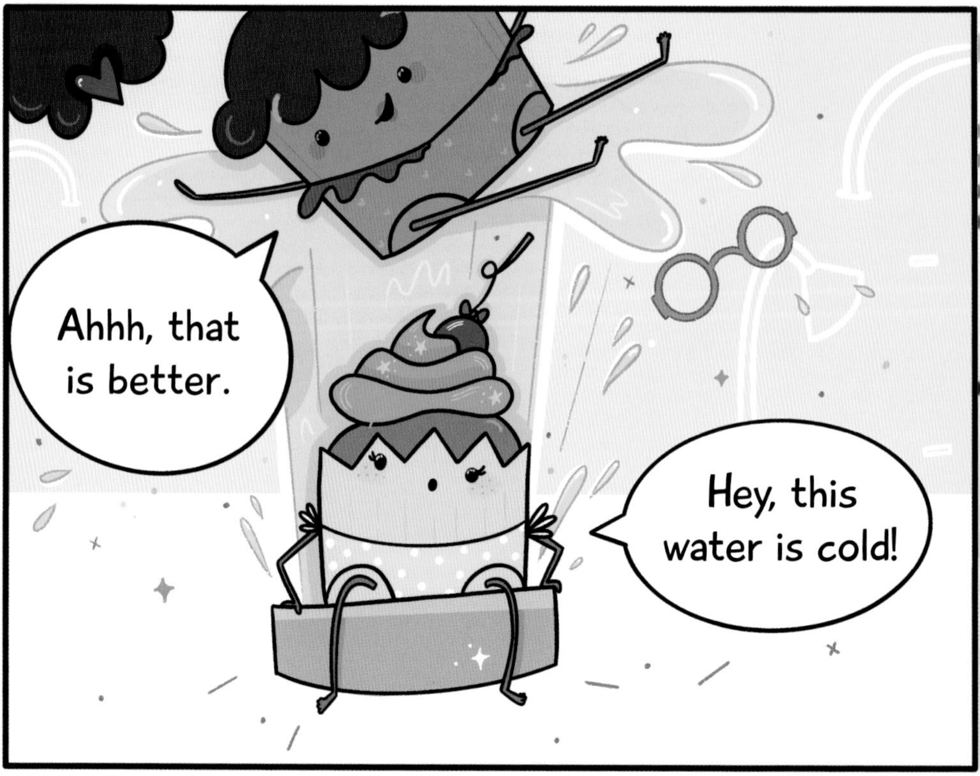
Ahhh, that is better.
Hey, this water is cold!

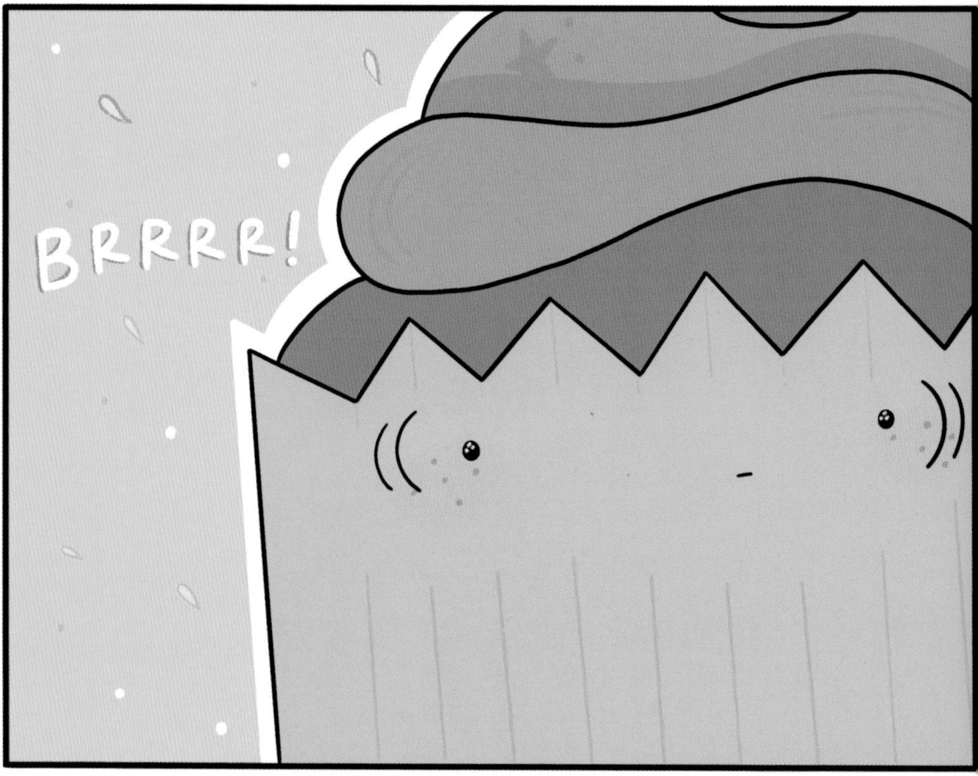
BRRRR!

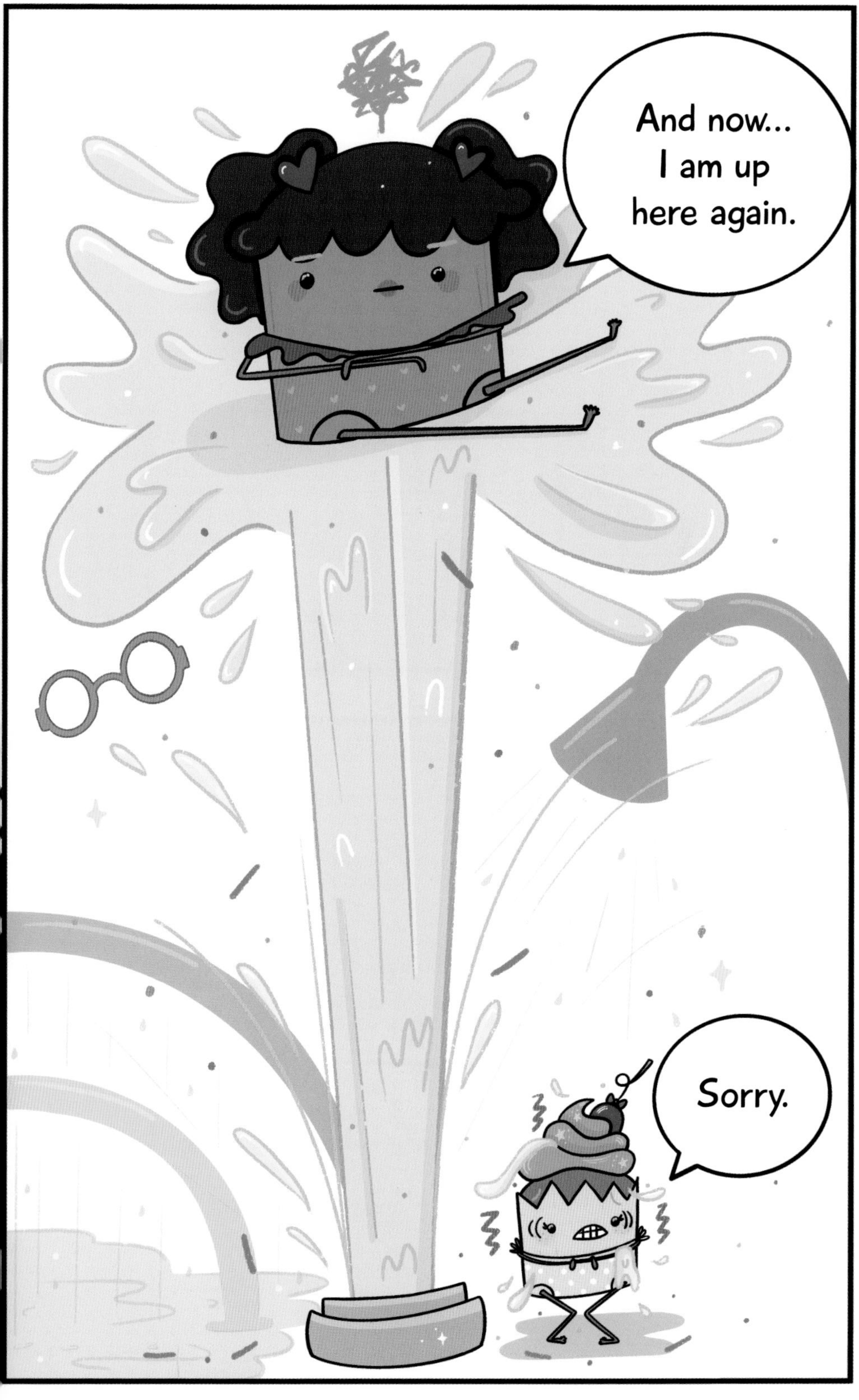
And now...
I am up
here again.
Sorry.

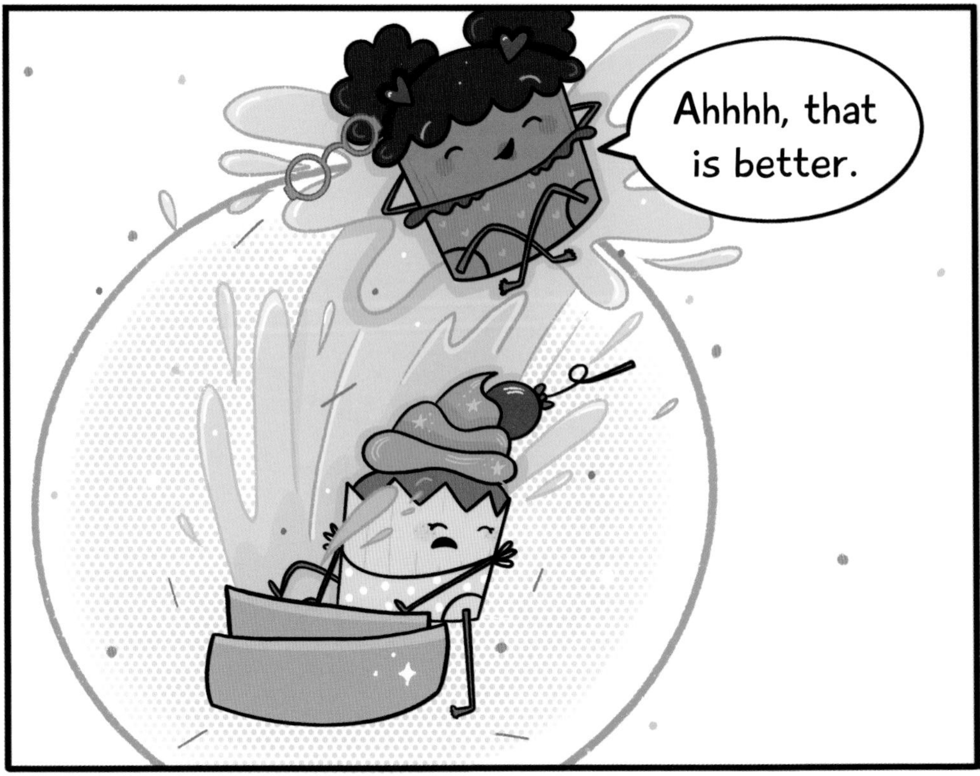
Ahhhh, that is better.

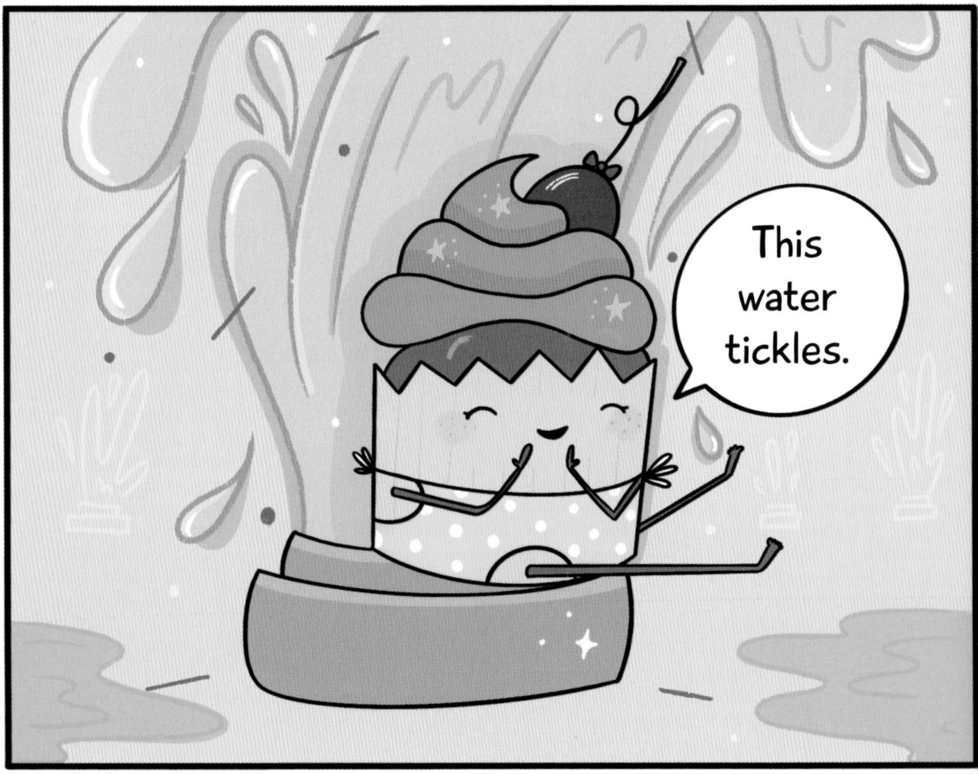
This water tickles.

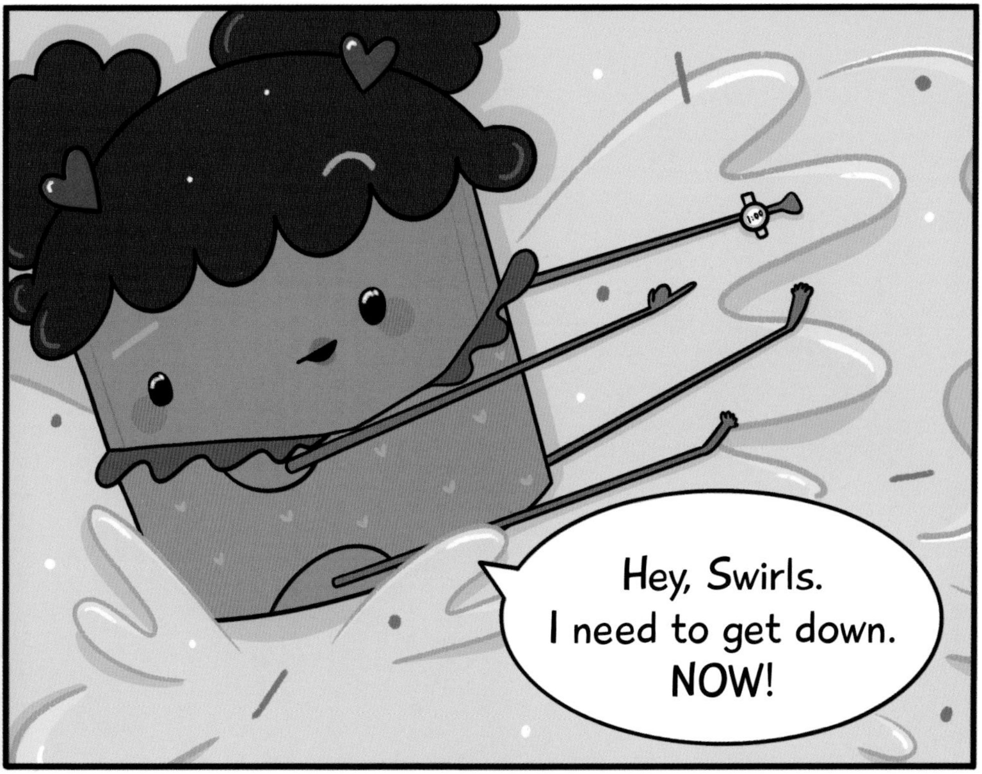
Hey, Swirls.
I need to get down.
NOW!

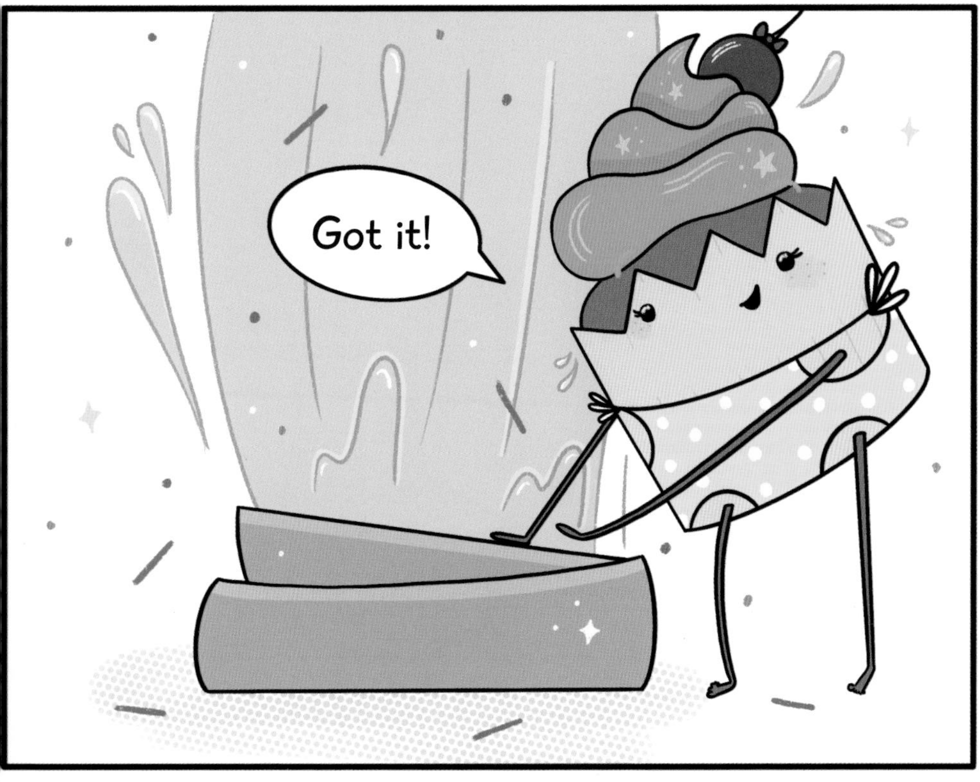
Got it!

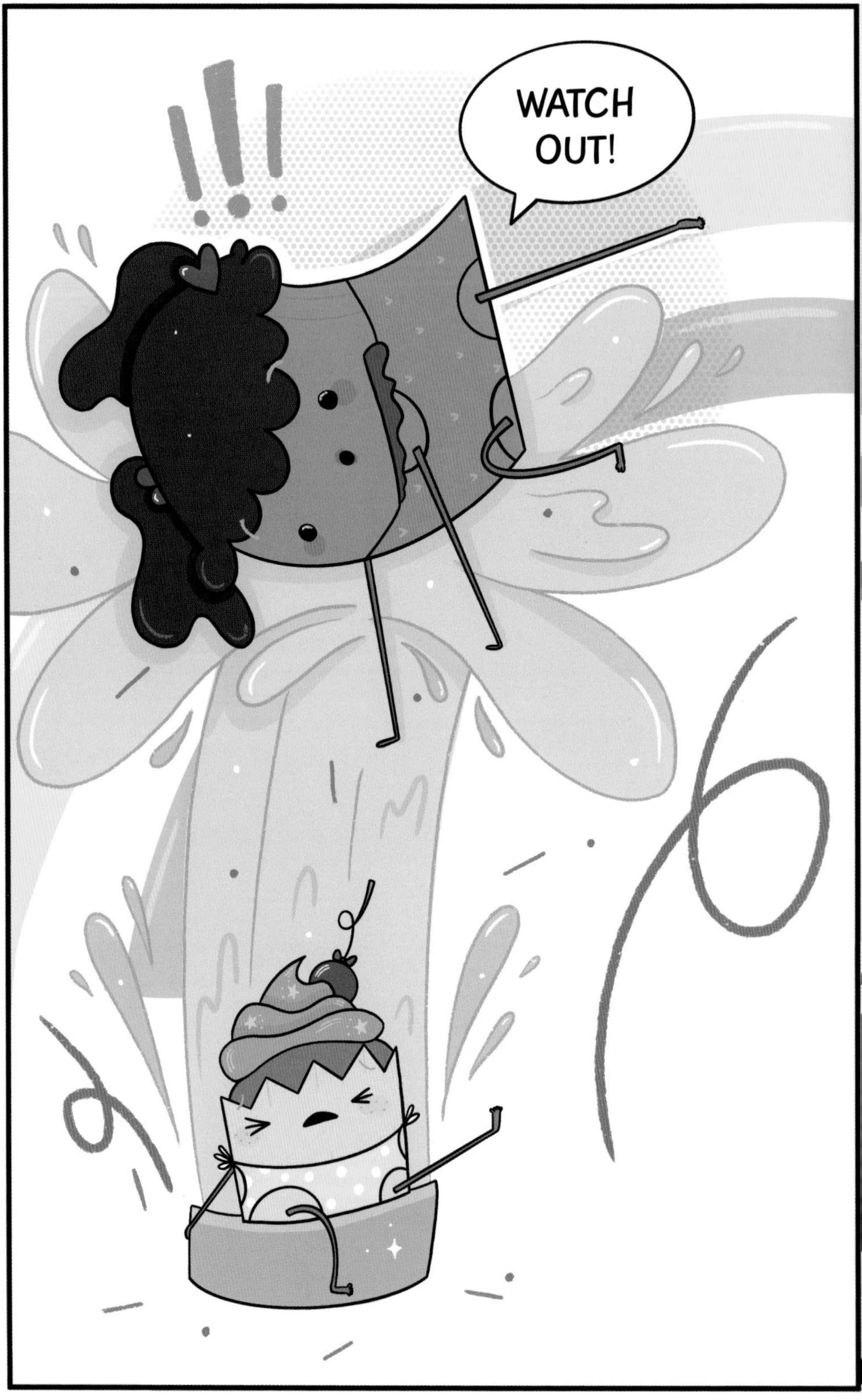
WATCH OUT!

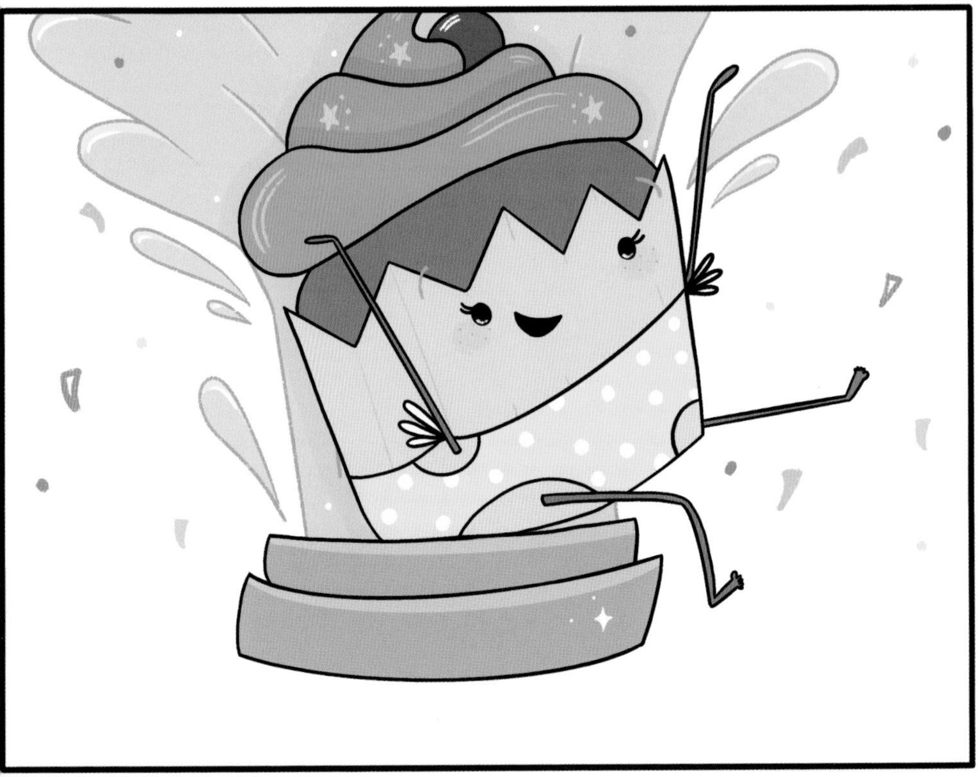

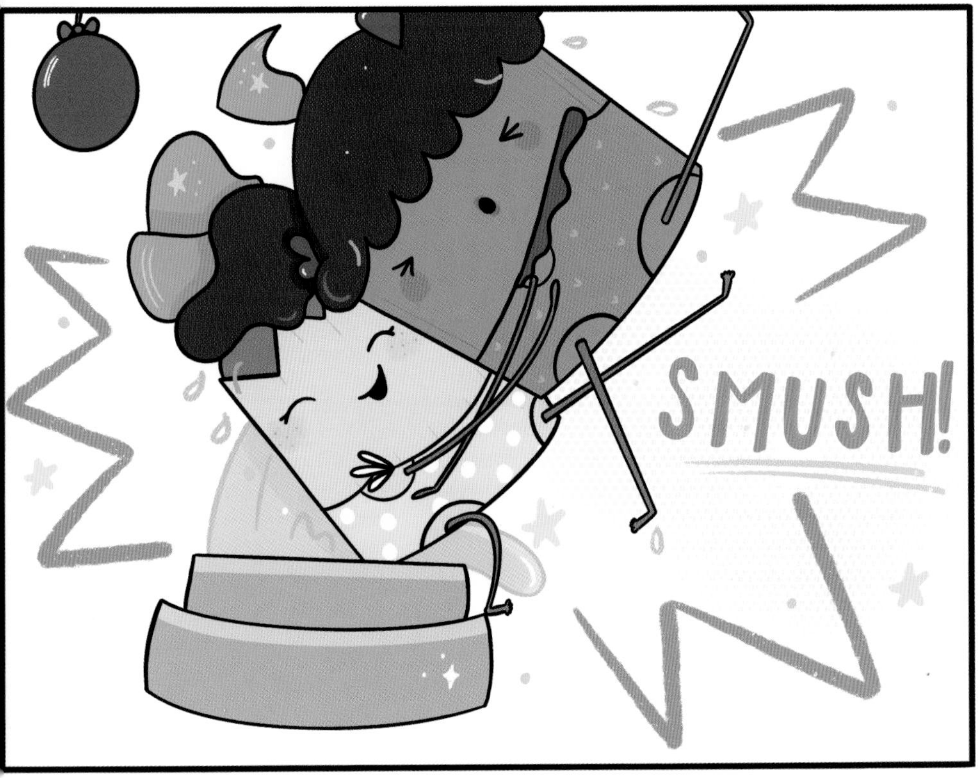
SMUSH!

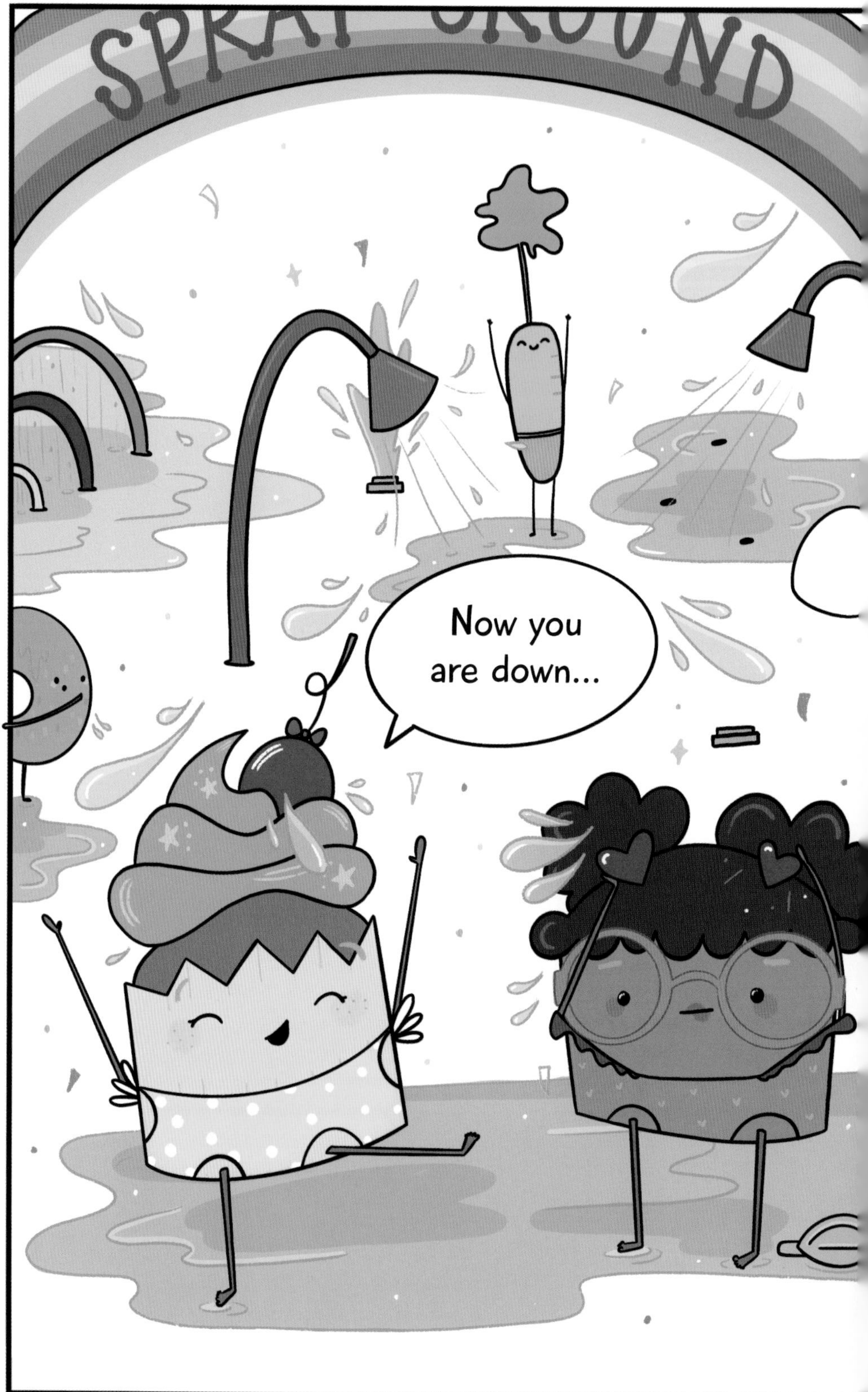
Now you are down...

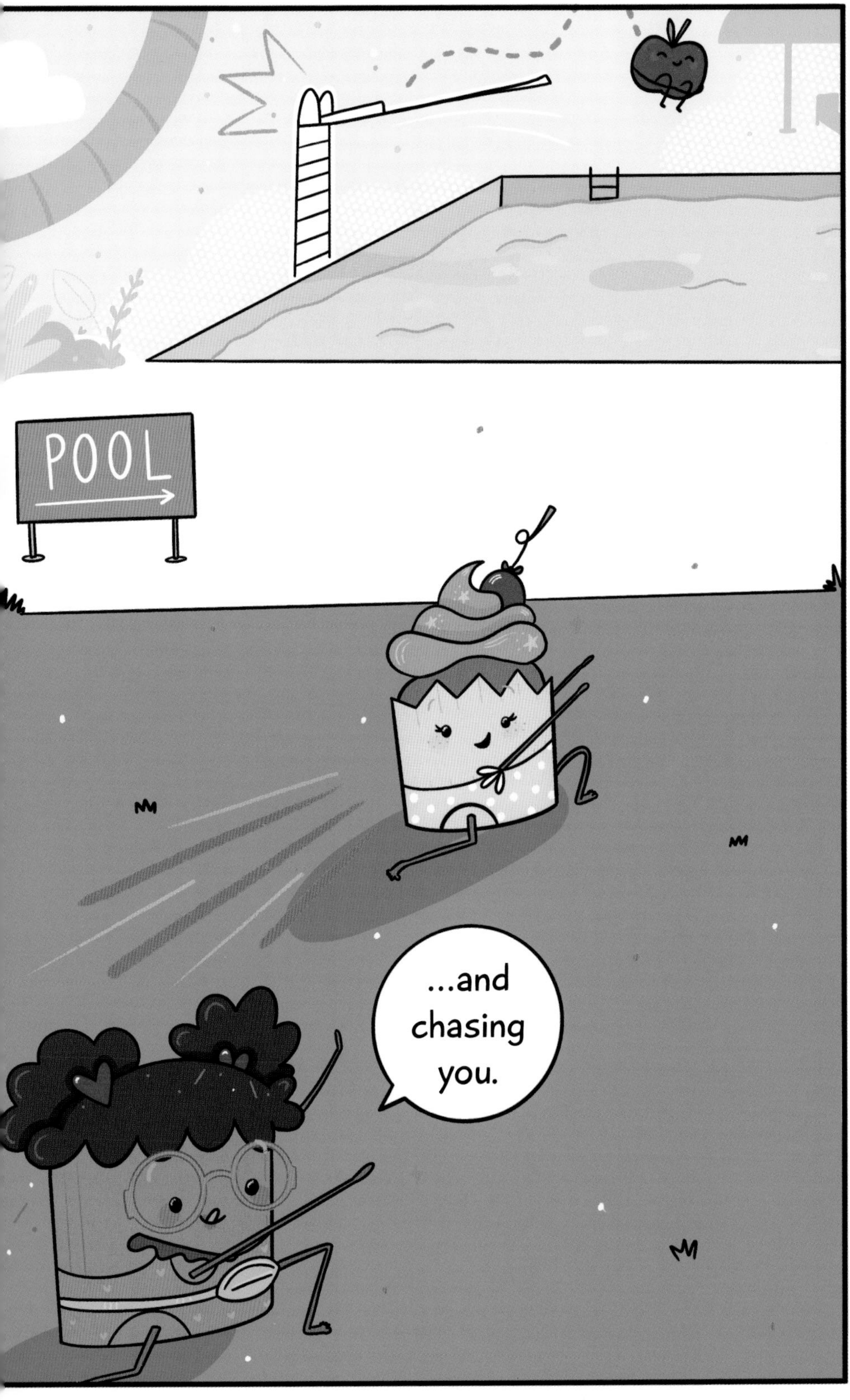
POOL
...and chasing you.

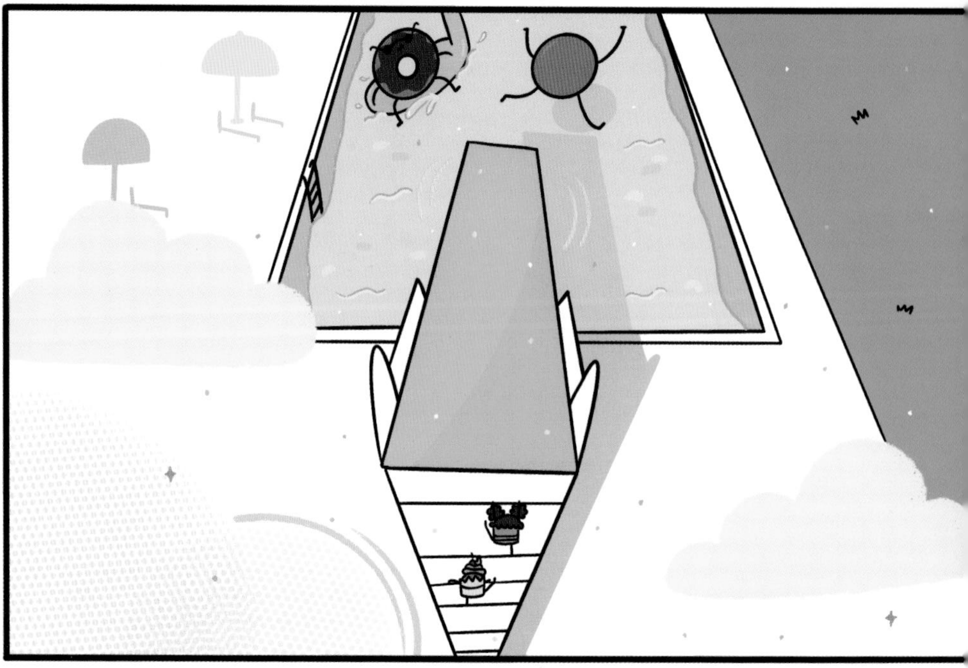

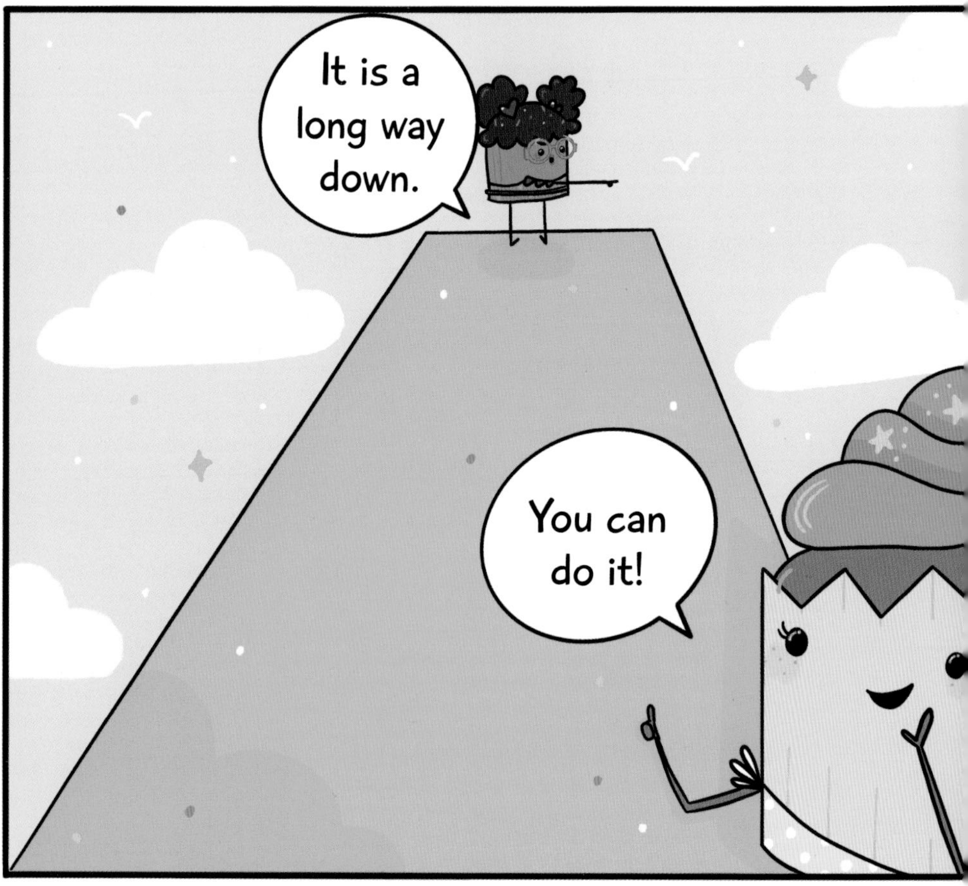
It is a long way down.
You can do it!

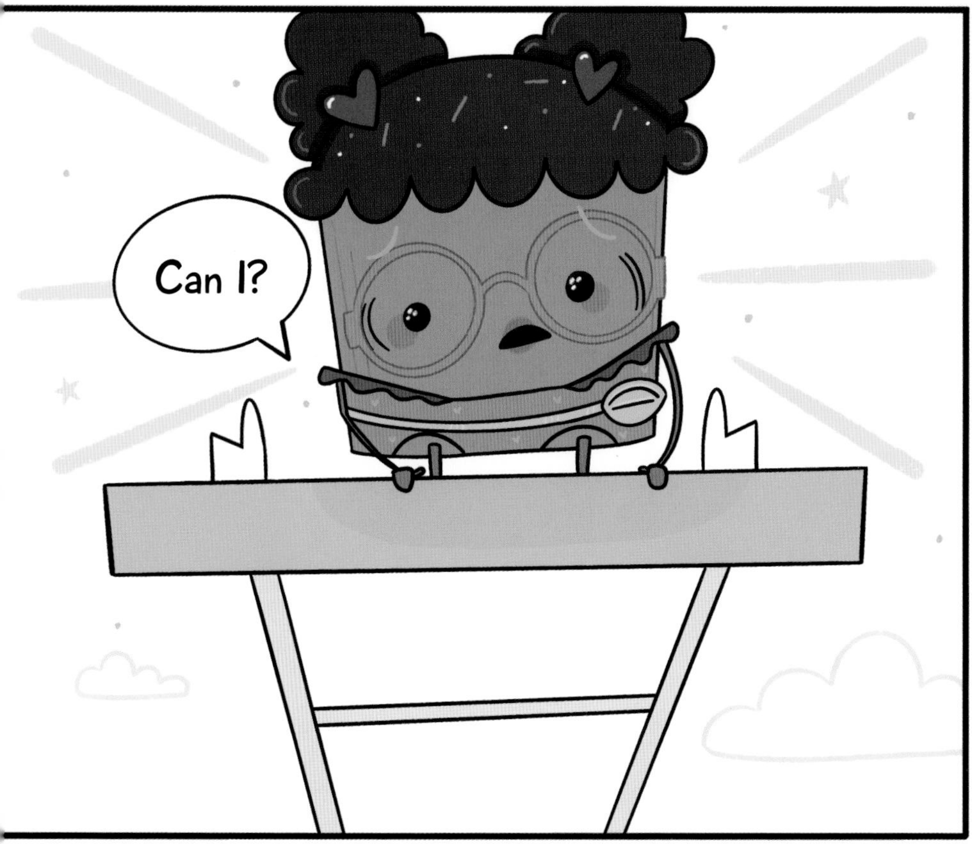
Can I?

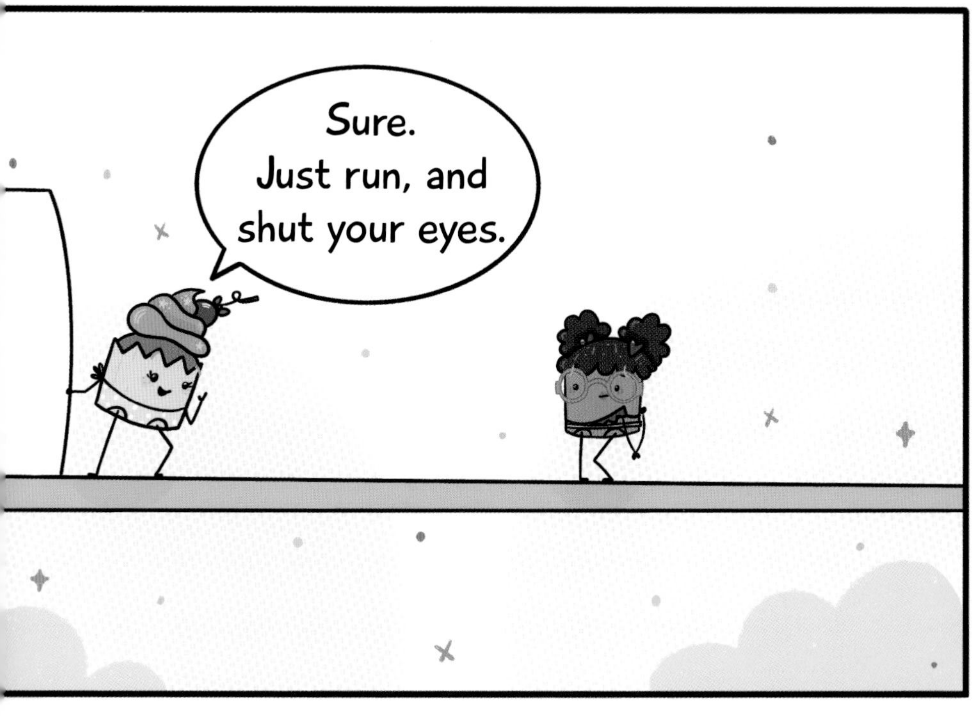
Sure.
Just run, and
shut your eyes.

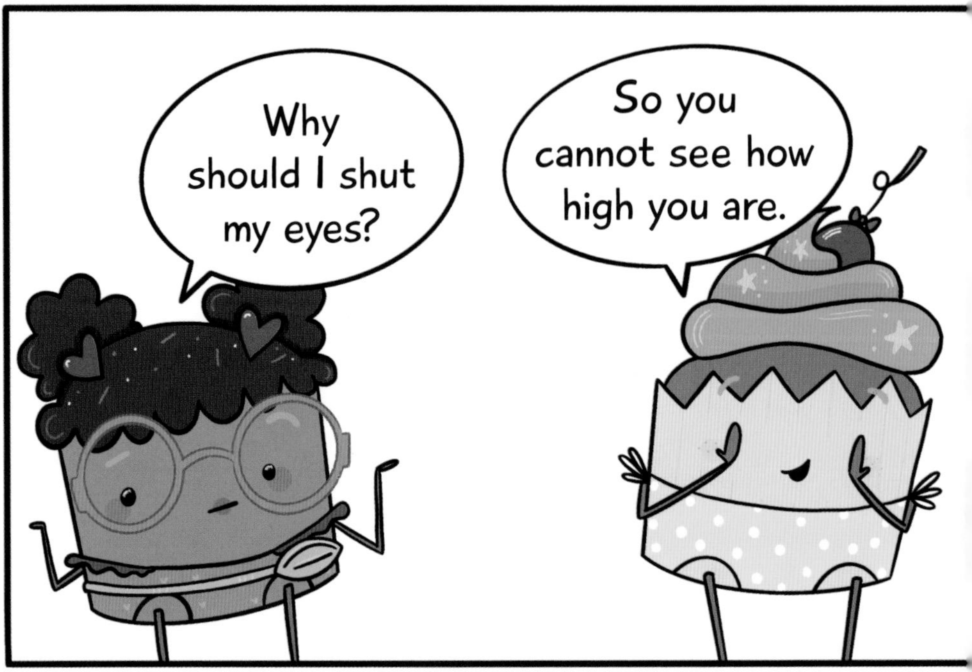
Why should I shut my eyes?
So you cannot see how high you are.

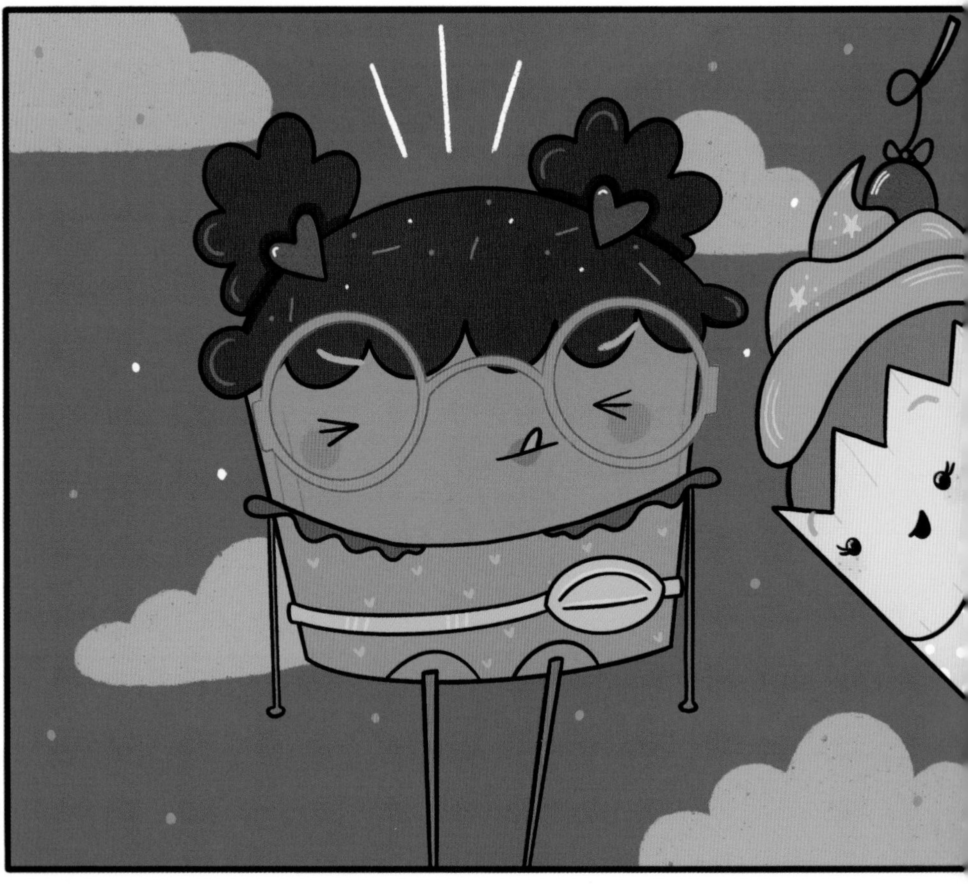

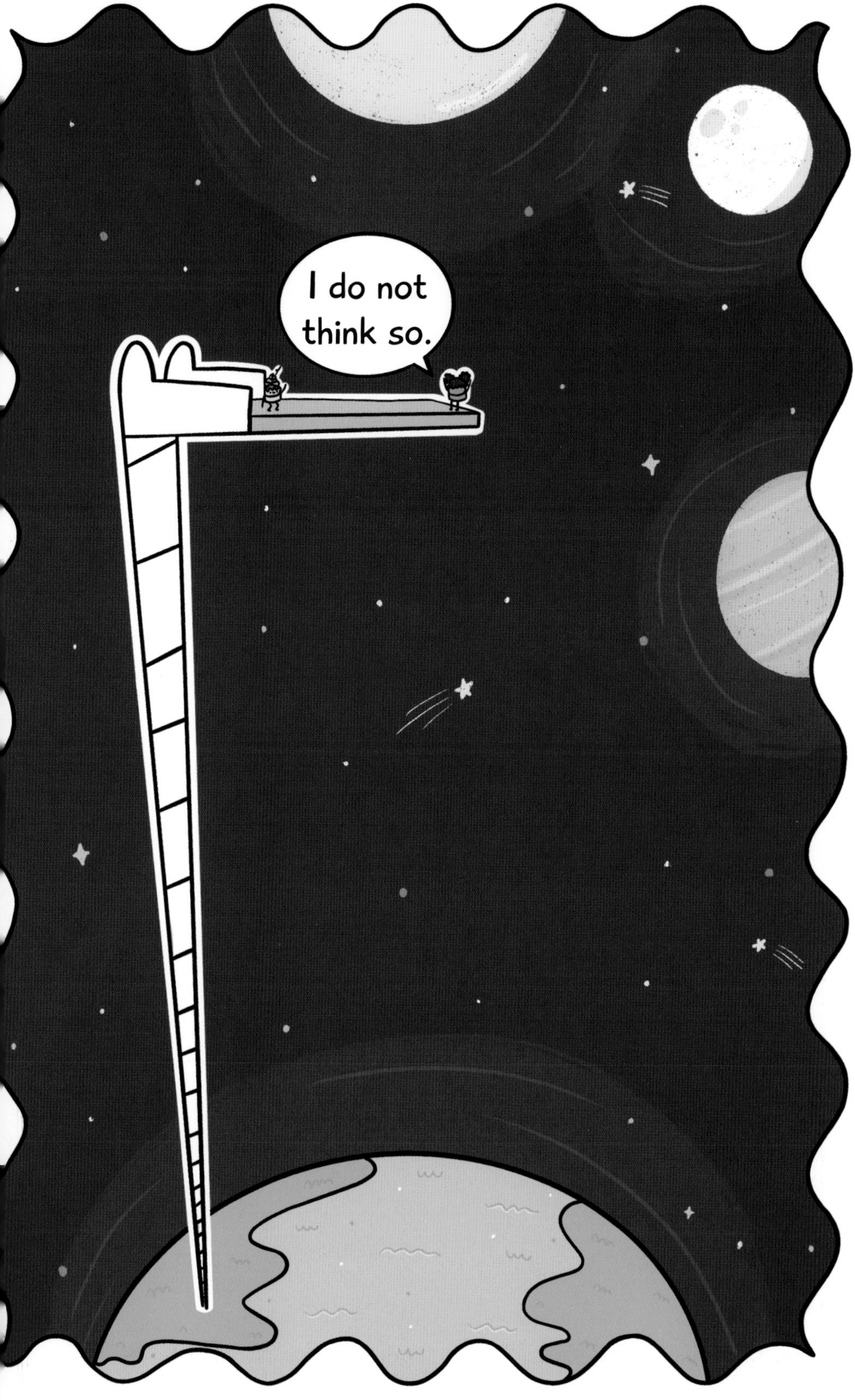
I do not think so.

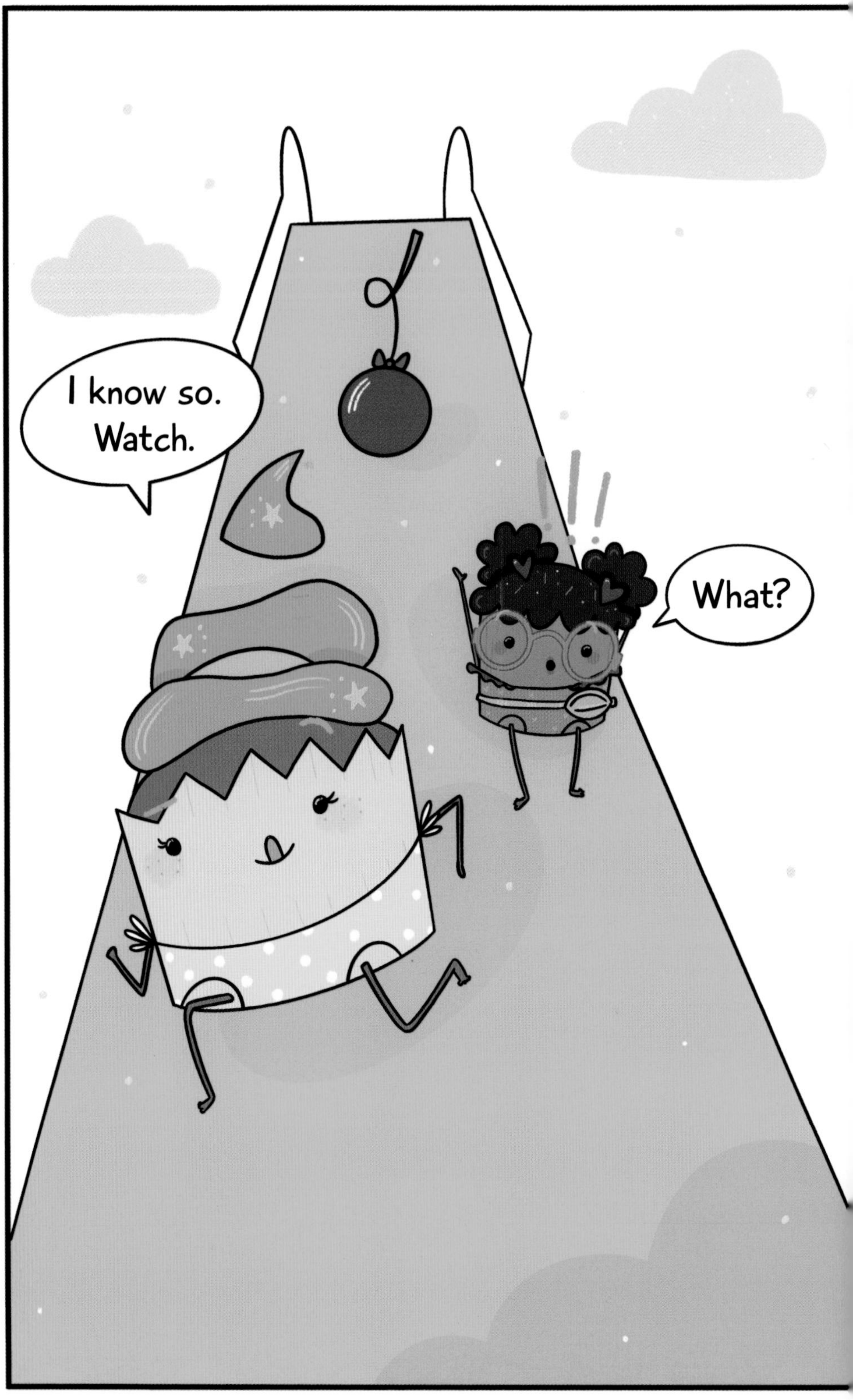
I know so. Watch.
What?

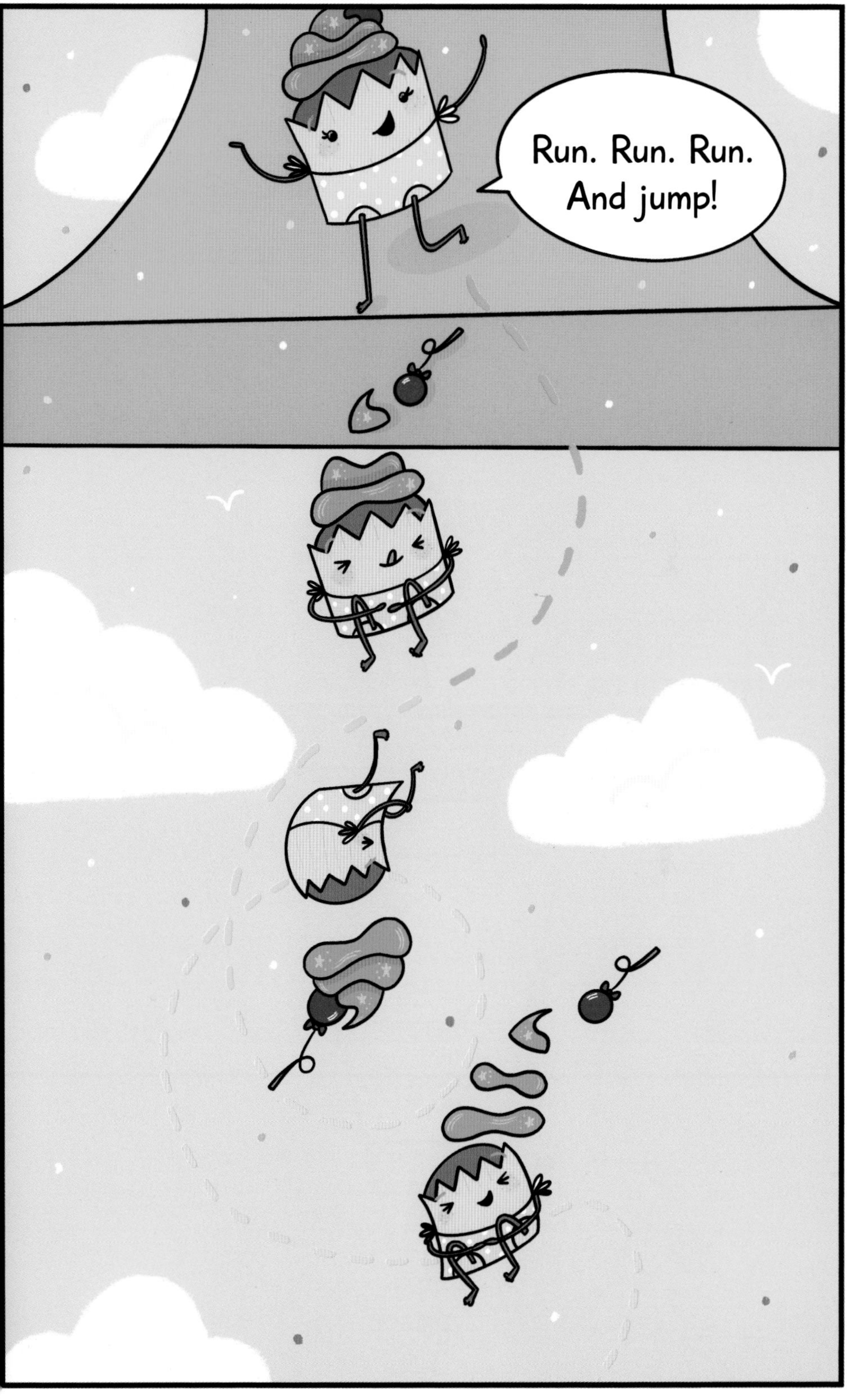
Run. Run. Run. And jump!

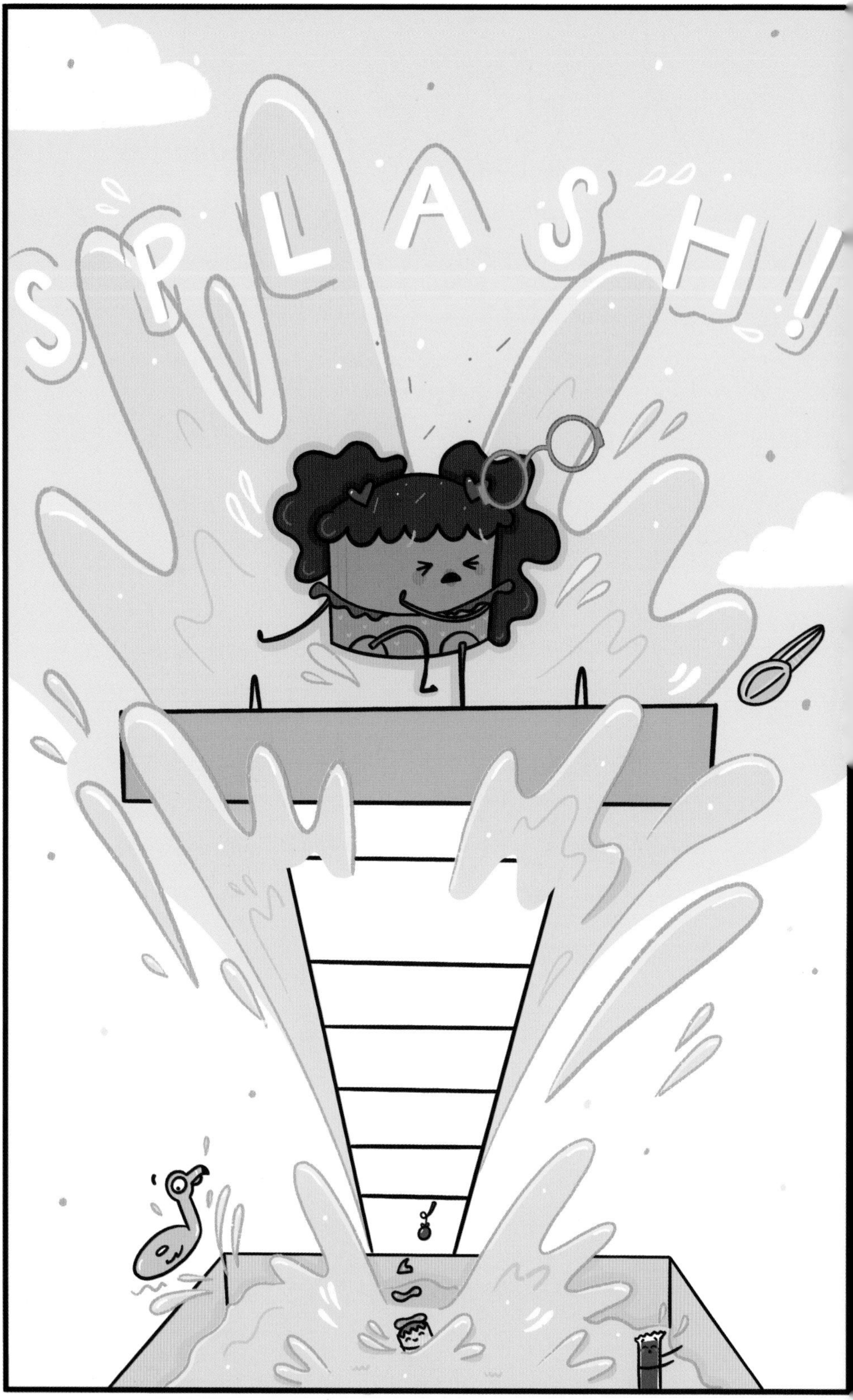
SPLASH!

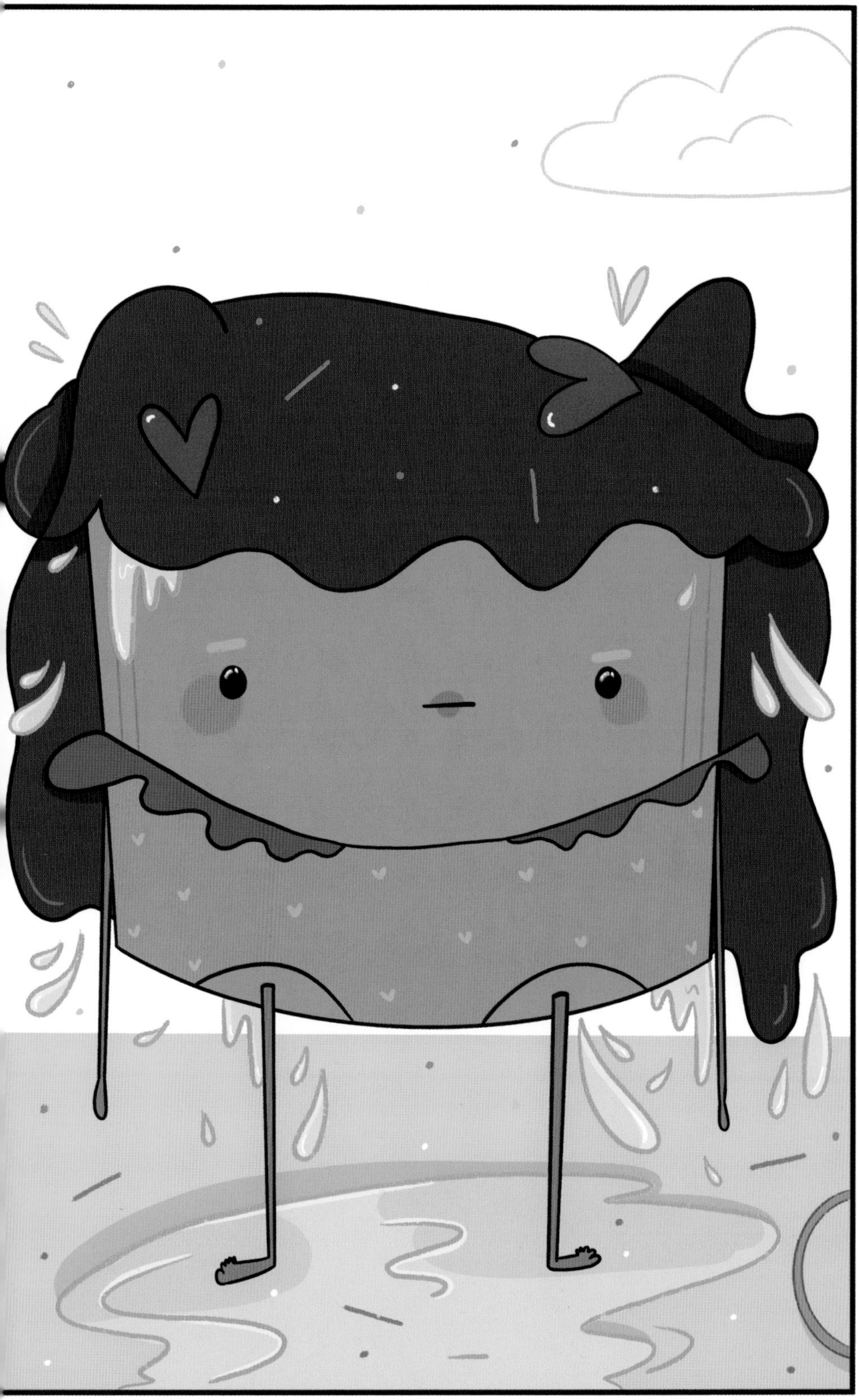

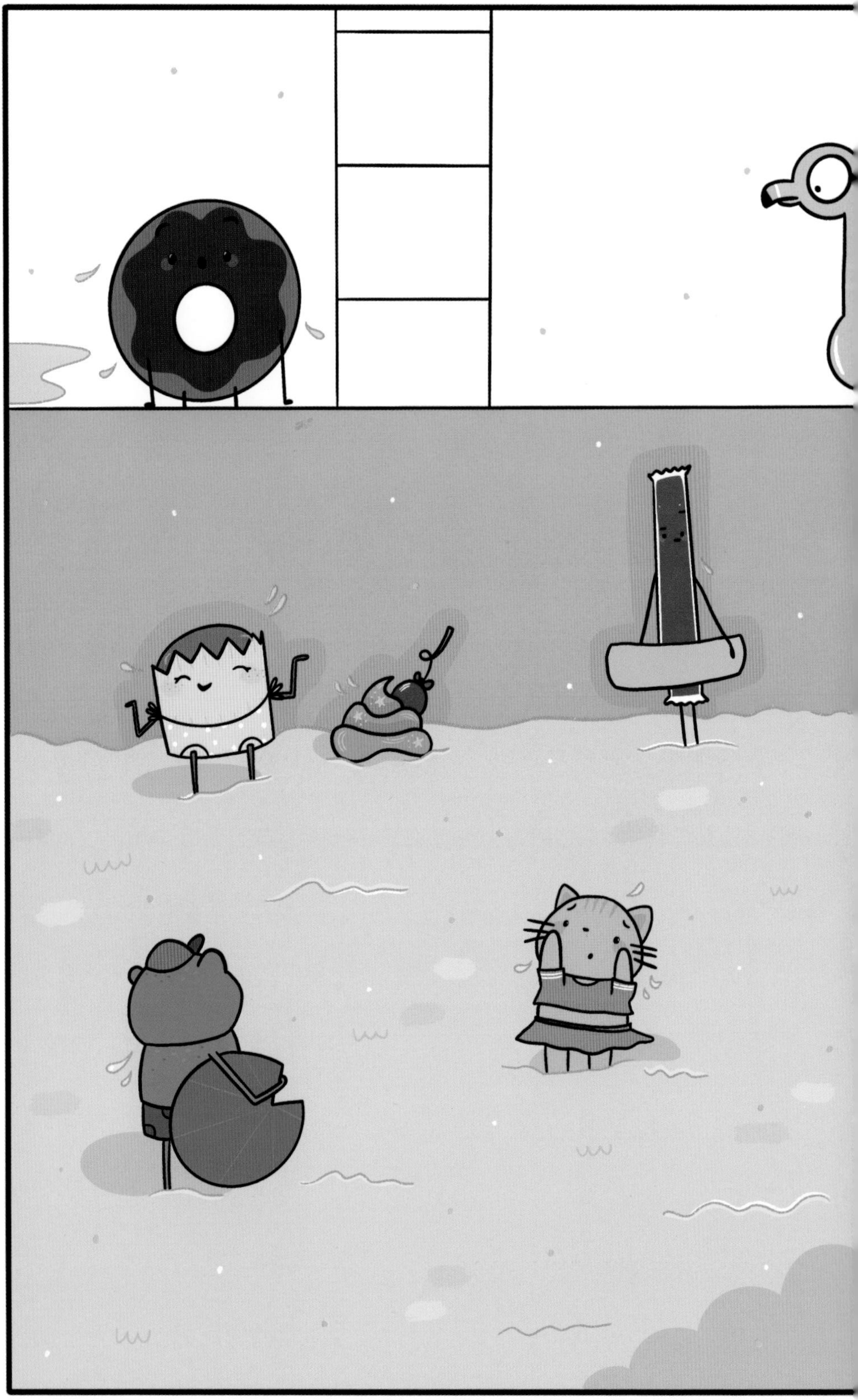

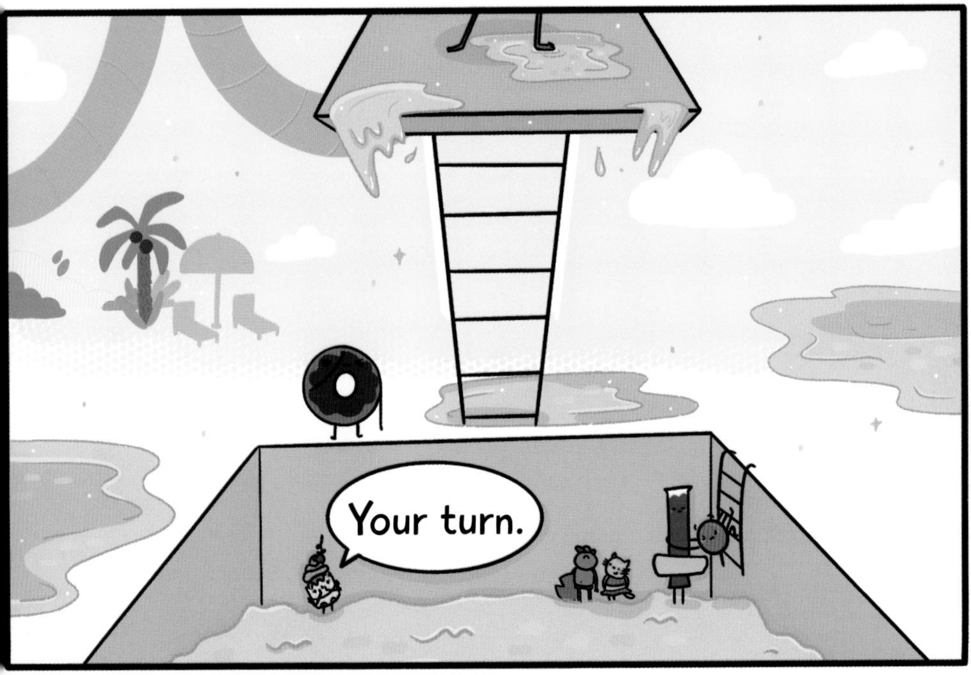
Your turn.

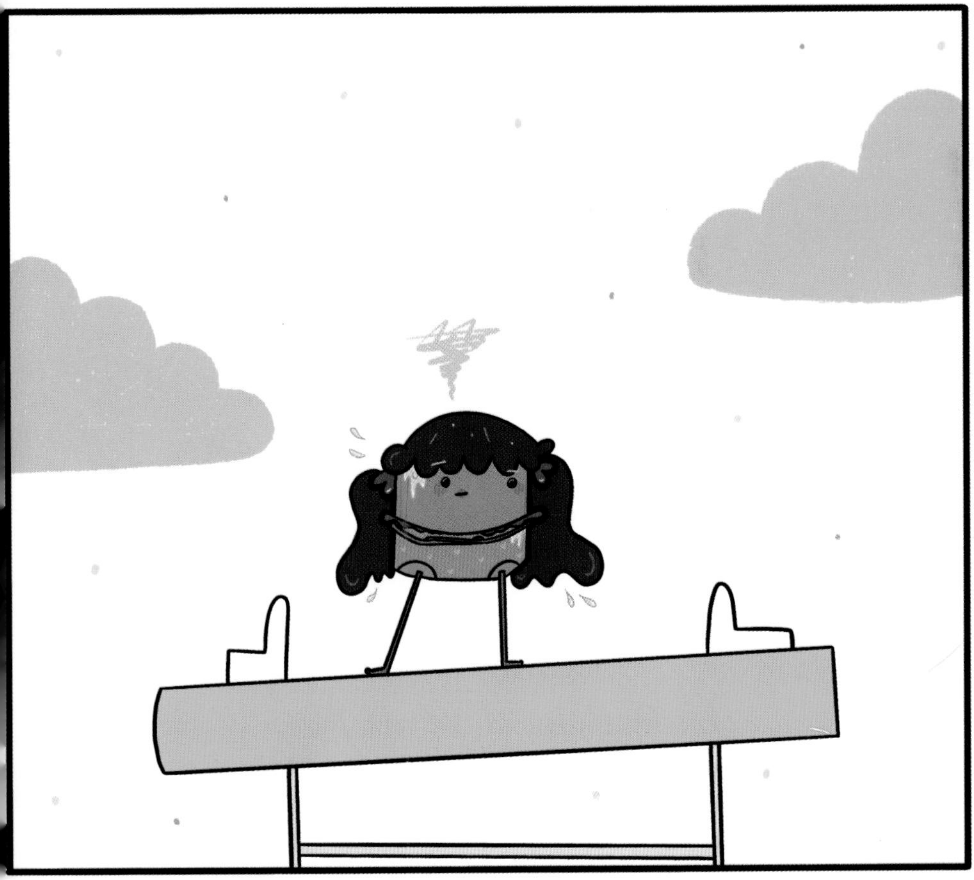

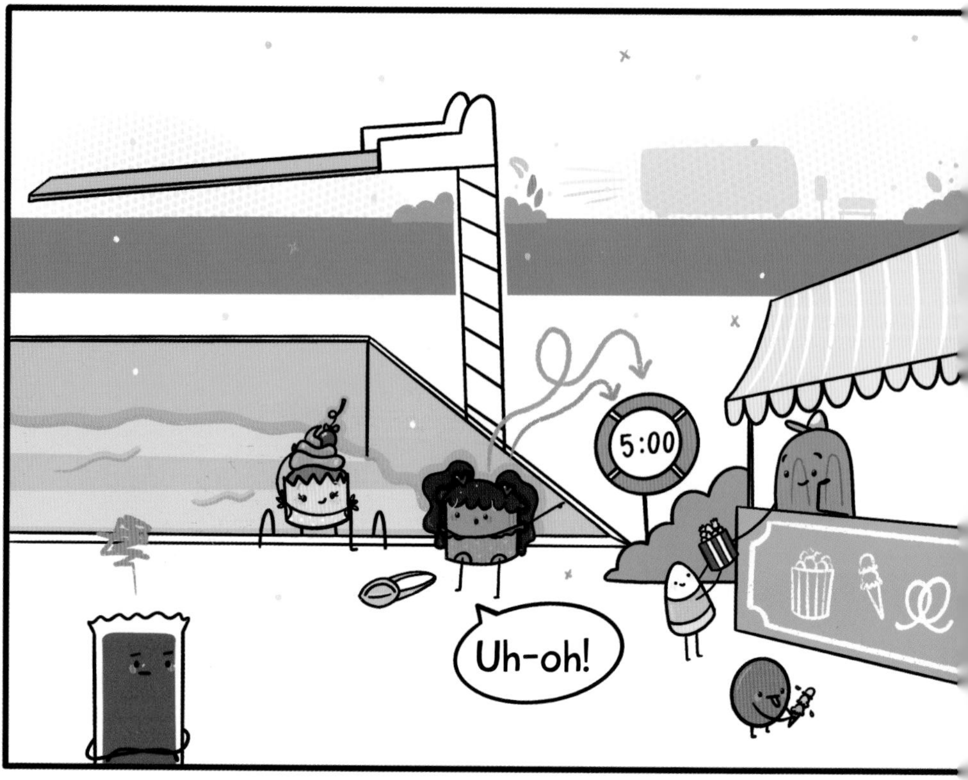
5:00
Uh-oh!

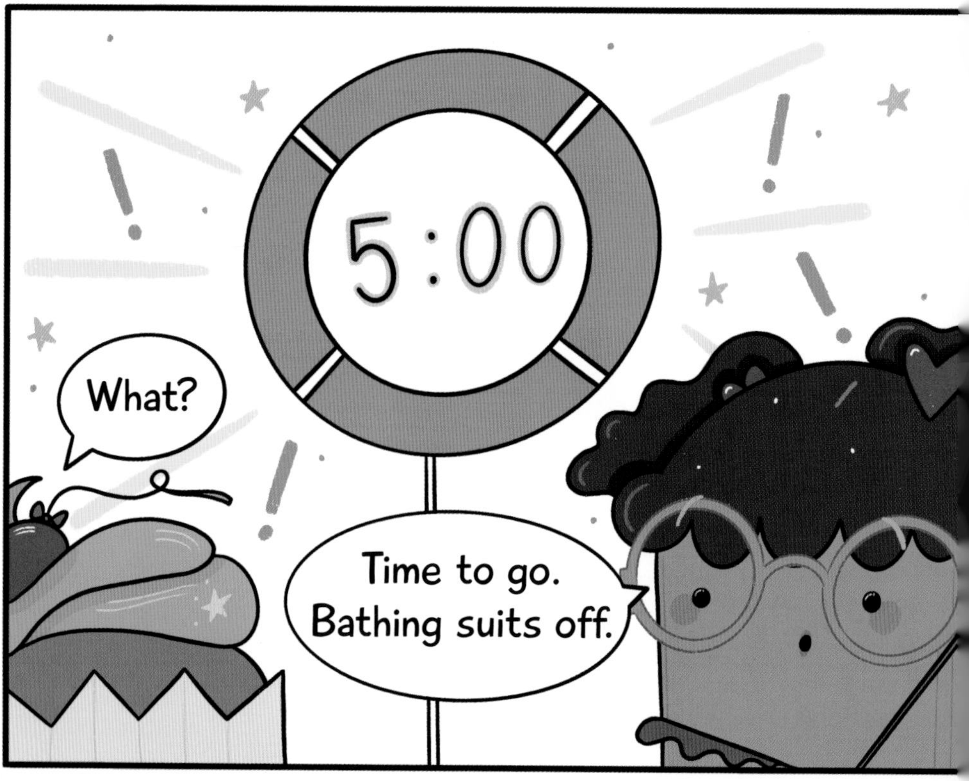
5:00
What?
Time to go.
Bathing suits off.

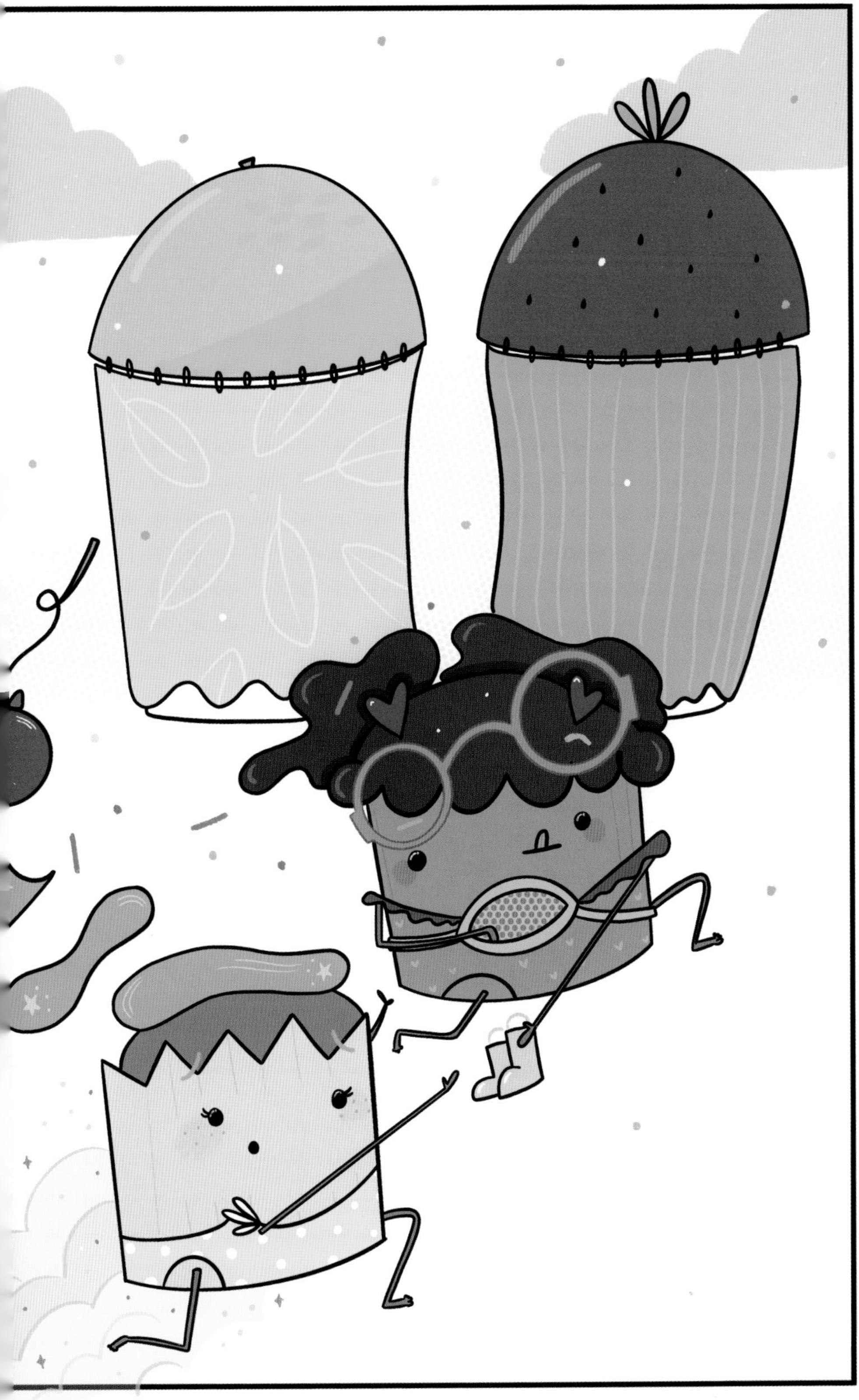

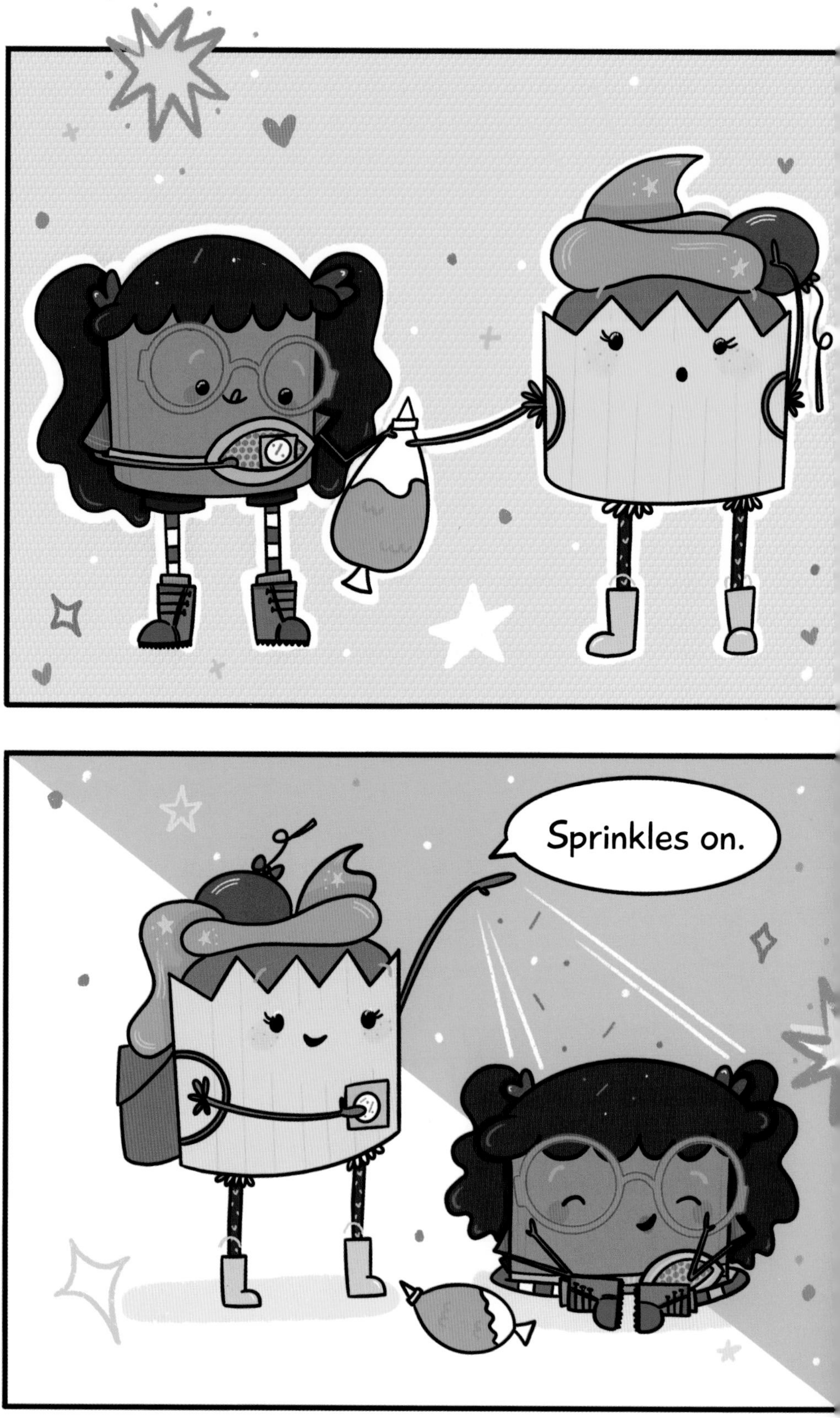
Sprinkles on.

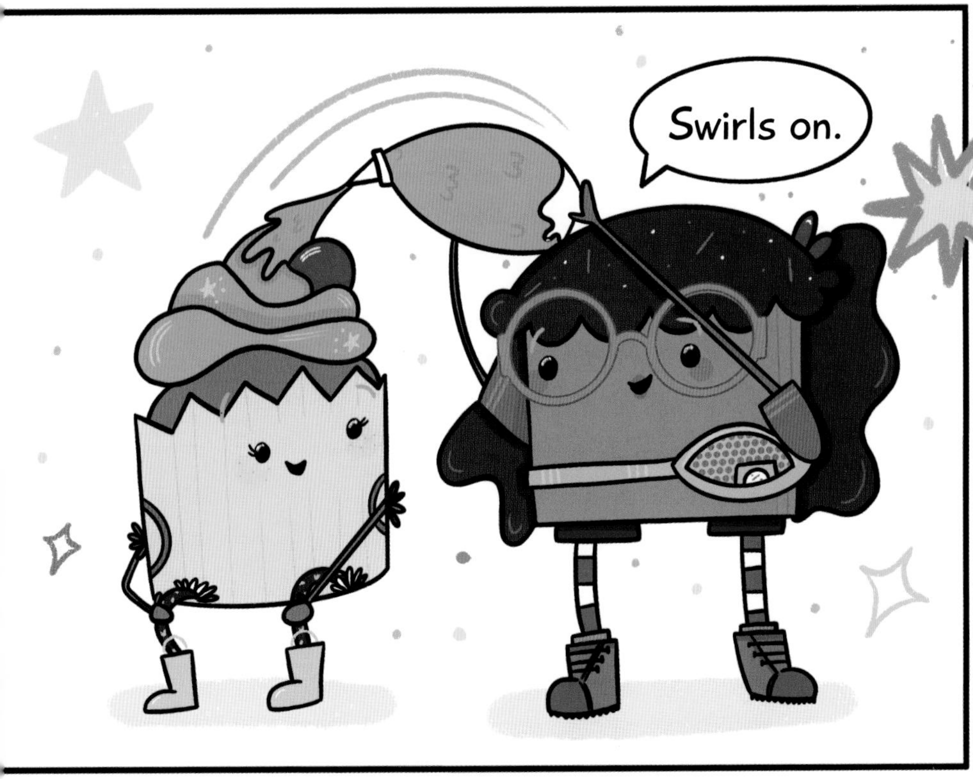
Swirls on.

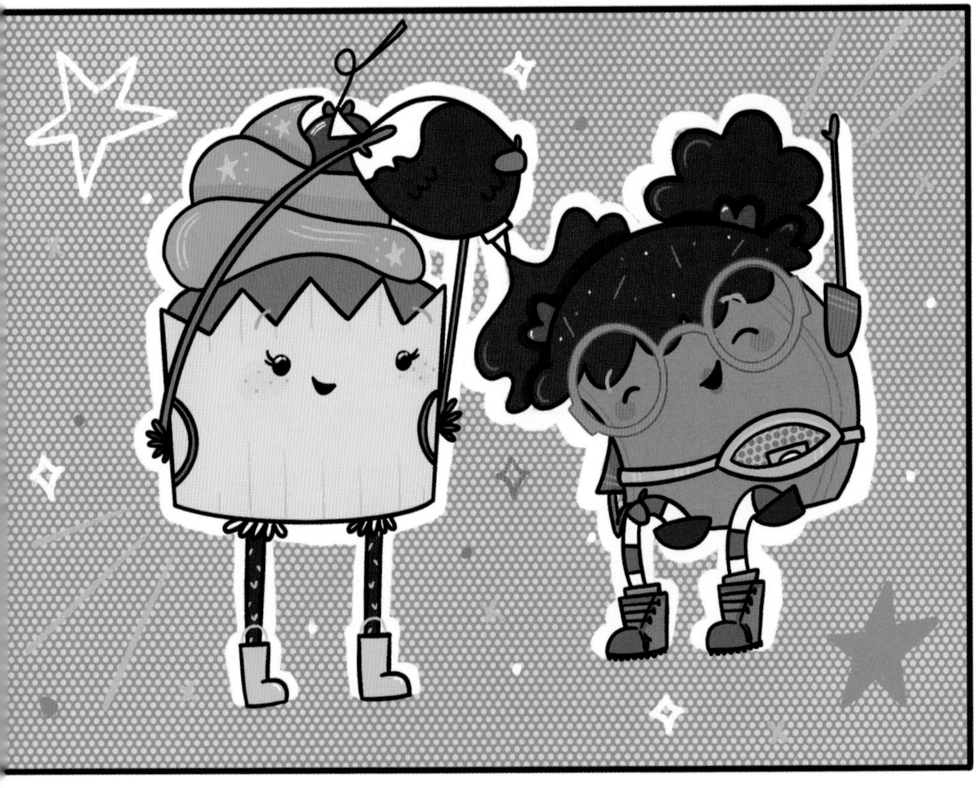

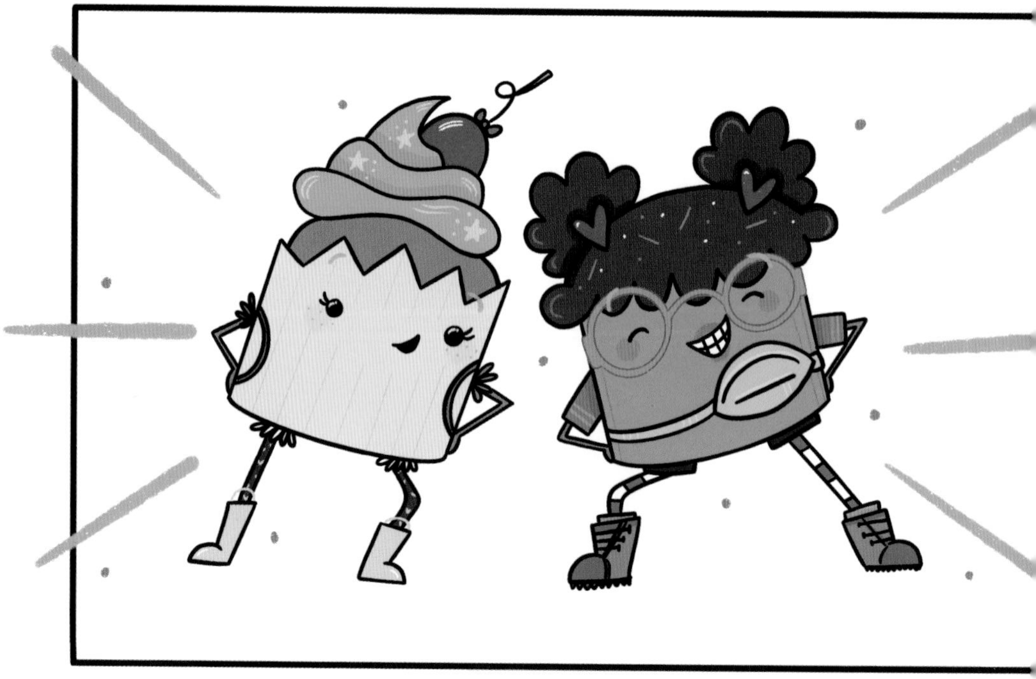

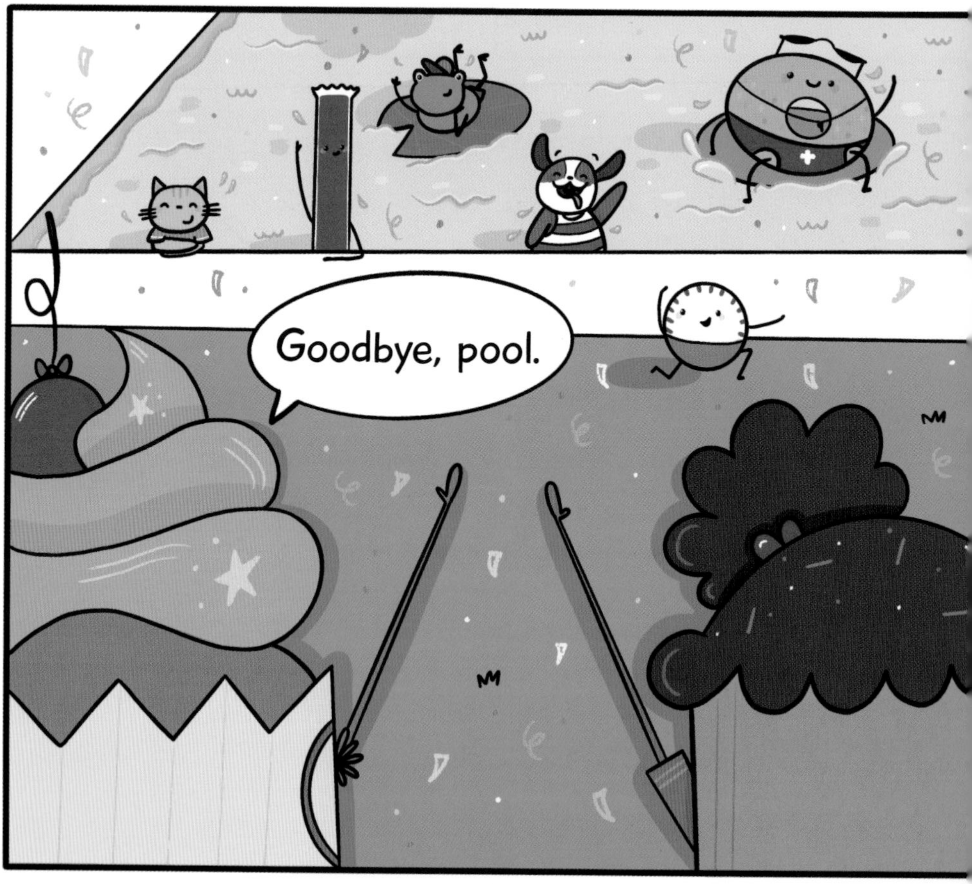
Goodbye, pool.

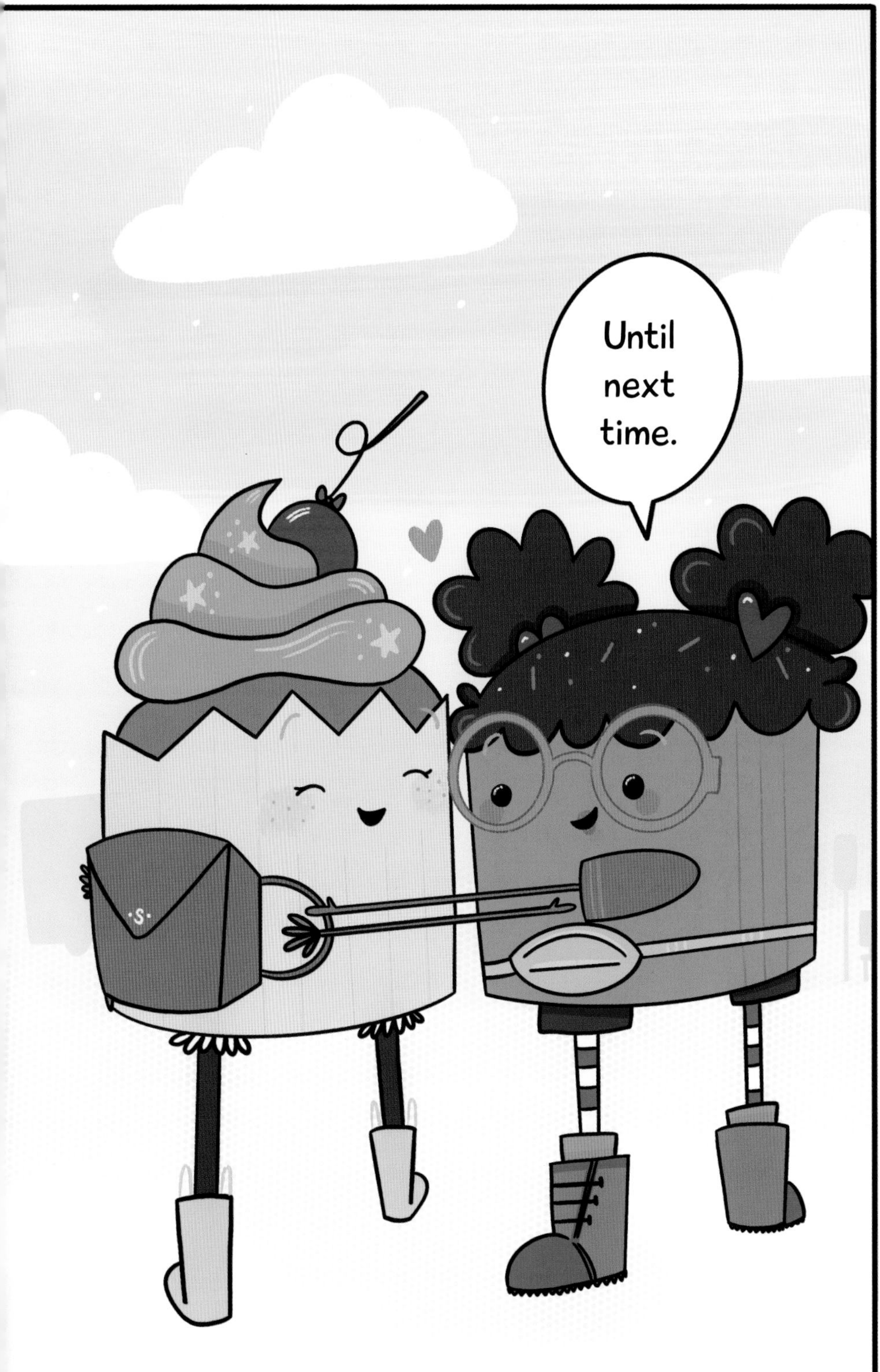
Until next time.

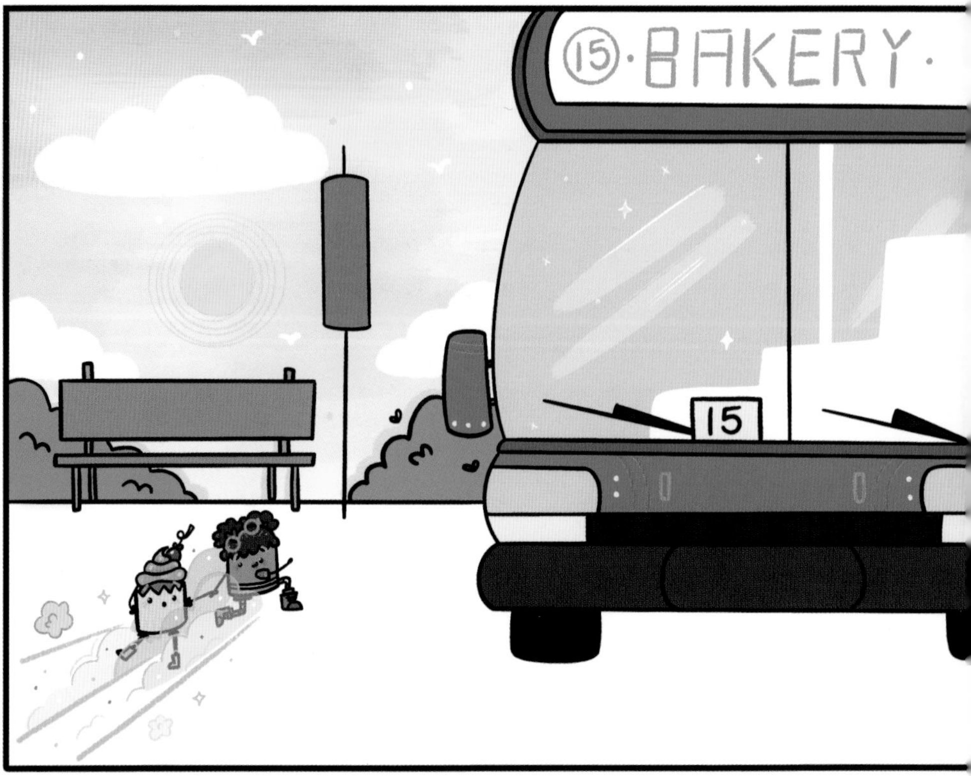
15 · BAKERY ·
15

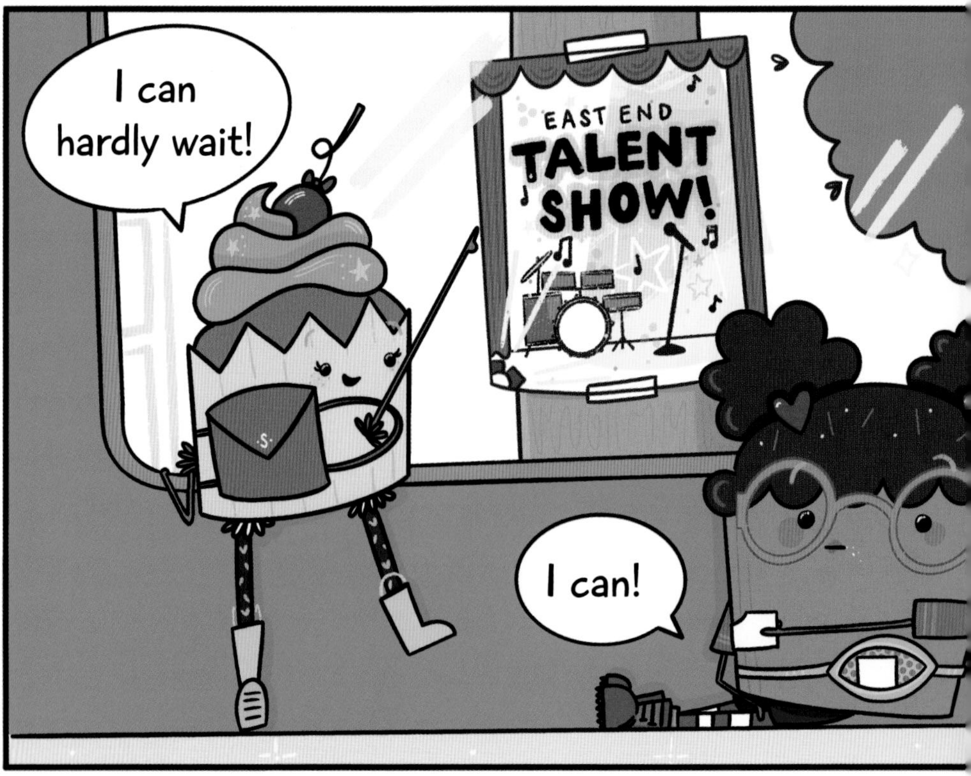
I can hardly wait!
EAST END
TALENT
SHOW!
I can!

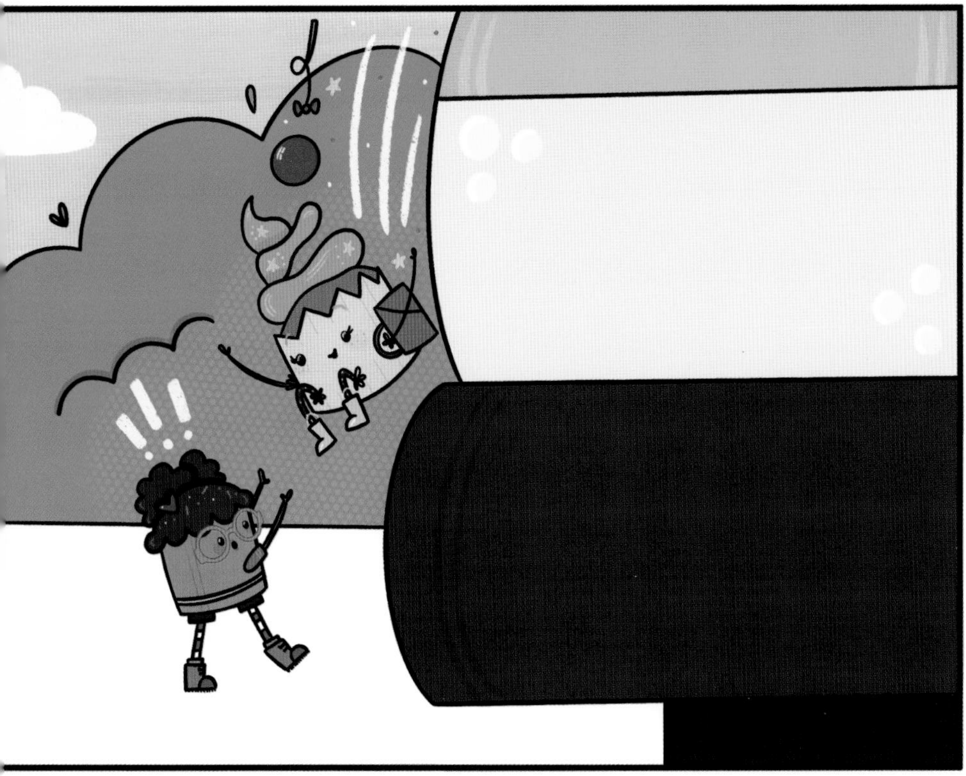
!!!

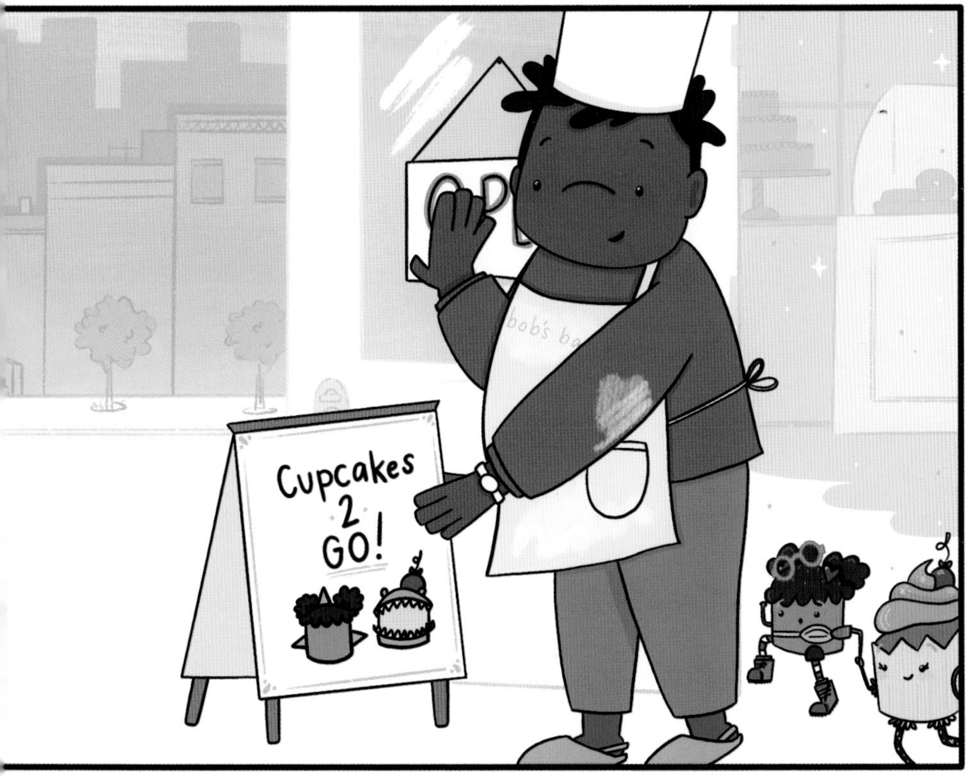
Cupcakes
2
GO!

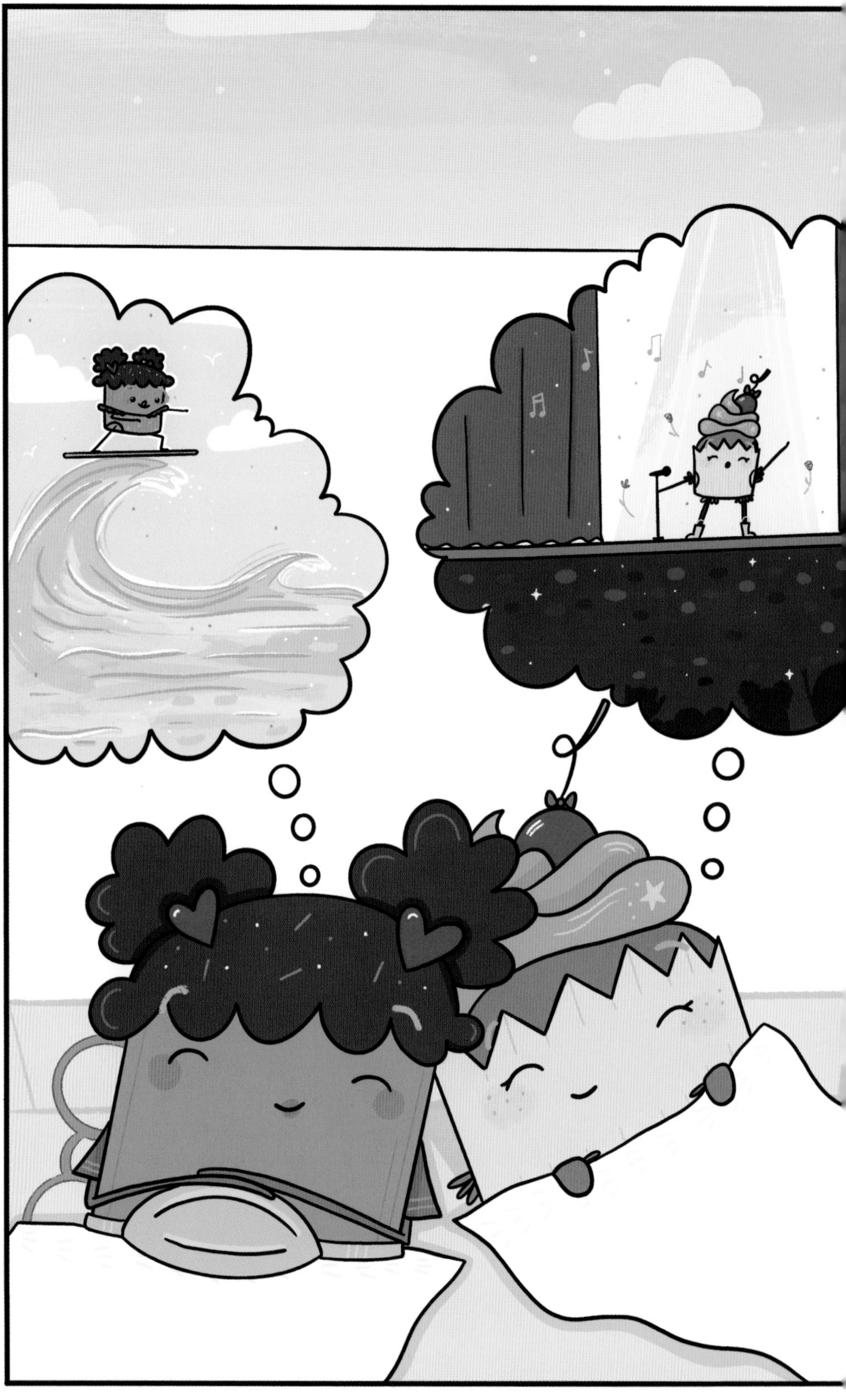